Levi's Ultimatum

ELIZA GAYLE

Visit Eliza Gayle at:

www.elizagayle.net

ACKNOWLEDGMENTS

There are many people who go into making each book the best it can be. Editors, cover artists, beta readers, critique partners and good friends. I owe them all so much.

Thanks to the patience and help of Cat Johnson, Selena Blake, Jessica Lee, Dahlia Rose and my family, I was able to finish this book and they helped me make it even better.

Special thanks to the beta readers Pamela S., Patricia S., Shayna S., Mary Ellen G, and Stephana B. who took the time to read from one chapter to the entire book and provide their opinion on how the story was going. Your input was invaluable.

LEVI's

ULTIMATUM

PROLOGUE

Mason Sinclair waited impatiently for Tucker to show up. He'd arrived early at Fire and Ice, the restaurant he and his partners had opened adjacent to the Purgatory club. He wanted to complete the mountain of boring but necessary paperwork that kept all of their businesses running smoothly. He was more than ready to get back to his office and back to the more important deals he had on his plate. If only he could get Tucker's head out of his ass and into the correct game. The last couple of weeks had been nerve-racking to say the least. While he'd enjoyed watching Tucker leave his self-imposed exile and fall for this new woman, he abhorred the fact she came with a lot of public baggage.

He figured the next several weeks were going to be the challenge of his life. Tucker would keep his mouth shut, but they simply didn't need anyone digging into his past.

Finally he noticed Tucker come through the front door, greet the hostesses with a hug and a smile before he made his way to the back room of the restaurant and took a seat across from Mason in one of the smooth leather booths.

They'd agreed to meet here because it afforded both

of them a decent amount of privacy. At this early hour not too many Doms had made their way to this area so they wouldn't be distracted by the lure of a scene to watch. Tucker glanced across the space to the table he'd occupied with his new sub, Maggie, only a couple of weeks ago. Mason may not have witnessed the event, but the staff had been all too happy to provide him with the lurid and juicy details.

"I see you managed to break away from the ball and chain."

Tucker flipped him off. "Whatever. You're just jealous you don't have a submissive right now."

"Oh is that all she is? Just another sub?"

"I think you know better than that."

They both knew better. Mason scrubbed his face and pushed back the fatigue weighing him down. Sleepless nights were not his friend. The years of secrets and separation had taken their toll on all of them, but he'd grown especially tired of trying to hold everything together. At the moment it all felt a little precarious. As if a threadbare string was all they had between normalcy and complete chaos.

The secrets were festering like a ticking time bomb.

"I need to tell her everything," Tucker blurted out.

"Jesus Christ, man. What the hell? Some of those secrets aren't yours to tell." His thoughts immediately went to Nina, the saucy sister, who'd suffered more than them all combined. When it came to Nina, Mason would protect her at all costs and God forbid if anyone got in his way.

"I'm going to ask Maggie to marry me as soon as we return from Boston. I can't start a marriage with lies and you know that."

Mason shrugged. "You already did, my friend. Marriage is merely a legal device and we both know the collar you put around her neck is far more meaningful.

You've waited all your life for her, but that doesn't mean it has to come at the expense of the rest of us."

Tucker winced. He knew Mason was right. He may have bound Maggie to him as his submissive, but when she found out he'd kept most of the truth from her, she might still run and then she'd be the mess that he'd have to clean up.

"We can trust her, Mace."

"Maybe." What little he'd seen of Maggie impressed him. She had quite a backbone for all she'd been through. Maybe because of it. "But are you willing to gamble with our lives to please her?"

"If you won't agree, then I'll have to talk to Levi and Nina. We can all decide together."

"Fuck that." Mason tried to hold his temper and failed. He clenched his hands into fists under the table.

Tucker glowered at him. "Don't even pull your shit with me. We're all in this equally. You are not the man in charge."

"Sure fooled me. I'm the one who's been keeping our shit together for years," he grit through clenched teeth. "Don't get me wrong, Tuck. I'm thrilled you've made so much progress in your life. No one deserves it more. But I've worked my ass off making sure no detail fell through the cracks when it came to the lives and welfare of *everyone* involved. Do you have any idea what that entails?"

"I'm not an idiot. Unfortunately the best-kept secrets are still secrets and one day they're gonna explode in your face. Like that reporter. Have you heard anything more from her?"

Mason's eyes darkened and a scowl crossed his face. "She's still here and nosing around, but I'm handling it. If things get any worse, I have a plan B."

Tucker studied him for a moment.

Mason pulled his eyebrows together. After a few

seconds he leaned back and crossed his arms over his chest. He wasn't going to allow Tucker to psychoanalyze him.

"Plan B, huh? You must be worried."

"I'm going to have to talk to her. The more she pokes the better likelihood she'll find something by accident, which is completely unacceptable." Of course the fact his dick got hard every time she came within a mile of him didn't help. He needed to schedule a scene at the club and get laid. Fucking had a way of clearing his head like nothing else.

"Maybe it's time for said contingency plan."

"If you've got another idea that doesn't include an orange jumpsuit for the three of us, I'm all ears." He was fresh out of ideas at the moment.

"I think it's time we talk to Levi. I've got a bad feeling about all this. Too much is happening all at once."

"Yeah, well--"

"What?"

Mason frowned. "Levi's gone missing. Again."

"Excuse me?"

"I'm certain I don't need to repeat myself."

"God dammit, Mason. Stop with the macho bullshit. I am not above beating the ever living crap out of you."

A sardonic smile crossed his face as he thought about flexing his muscles in a good old-fashioned fist fight. "I'd love to see you try."

Tucker narrowed his eyes in warning. "Tell me about Levi. How do you know he's missing?"

"Because I've been looking for him for three weeks."

"That's why you came back here. This isn't about the reporter at all."

Mason hesitated. He'd been on his own making all

the decisions for so long it wasn't easy to confide in someone else. Not even Tucker. One of the few people on this earth he called friend. "Look, don't get crazy. The reporter thing is real, but yes, part of what drove me back here was the hope that I'd find Levi back in his hometown."

Tucker straightened in his seat and leaned forward. "What do you know?"

Mason sighed. A lot of what ifs were still running rampant through his mind. "It looks like he went off the grid about a month ago. As far as the investigator I hired can tell, he packed a bag, closed his house up and hit the road."

Tucker relaxed a fraction. "So he went on vacation?"

"Maybe. Wherever he went, he didn't want anyone to know. He's not used any of his credit cards or his cell phone. Although he never uses that damn phone. He avoids communication as much as possible. I'm beginning to wonder if his head will ever be in the right place again." Not to mention his gut told him something was up.

"I don't like this. Things have been quiet for years and now it's pure chaos. You get the impression things are unraveling?"

"I'm sure Levi will show up sooner or later." He wasn't going to feed Tucker's paranoia. He might be right, but the less he worried the more chance he'd keep the information to himself.

"It's not just Levi I'm worried about. Things are changing and if we don't change with them this isn't going to end well."

"Right now most of the change is coming from you. Maybe you ought to think about that. Although some change is inevitable." Mason stood, pulled out his wallet and laid down some cash for the drinks he'd consumed. "You've always had a flair for the dramatic, but for our sake I hope you're wrong this time."

When Tucker gave him a hard look, Mason laughed and gathered up his papers. The man was leaving town. That hopefully bought him a little more time to get a few fail-safes in place before everything blew up in their faces.

For now, Mason had a lovely submissive reporter who probably didn't even realize just how submissive she was waiting to meet with him. He'd begun circling the issue and working his way toward a new solution.

This is what he did. Cleaned up the messes his partners in trouble created. This time, however, he had more than his freedom at stake...

ONE

Levi clung to the side of the mountain by his fingertips while staring into the vast caverns thousands of feet below him. The Utah sun burned on his face, the oppressive summer heat choking him while his arms shook and his muscles strained at the sheer effort it took to keep from plunging to his death. His heart raced and he panted for breath. But the adrenaline rush he'd looked forward to when he'd started the physically demanding climb never materialized. The crushing disappointment of not reaching that pinnacle tore through his chest. For a long moment he stared toward the ground and wondered what it would feel like to free fall to the bottom. Would his heart burst in fear of the end or would the exhilaration of the ride make him forget about his impending death? Or was it the path to freedom? There was nothing he longed for more. He didn't have a death wish but this close to the edge between heaven and hell left him with a lot of curious questions about what if.

For years he'd traveled the world going from one rush to the next. Even the time he'd spent in the Marines kept him on his toes and his mind somewhat focused. Then once again the toll of death during a deployment in Afghanistan, dug its claws into his gut and began twisting and taking root, threatening to tear him apart all over again. So he'd walked away when his contract had expired and moved as far from his past as he could get. He mostly spent time in third-world countries with his only contact to the past his emails and occasional phone calls from Mason and Tucker. The two men he'd gotten to know in college who had forever changed his life.

Twice in the last two years he'd contemplated going home again. Once he'd even driven to the North Carolina state line and stopped. After that, he'd remained stateside and gravitated toward the larger cities that offered a man pretty much anything he wanted as anonymously as possible. Until a month ago, with the darkness once again barking at his heels, he'd chosen to go completely off the grid. Day after day he'd gone from one place to the next looking for something that could obliterate the loneliness that continued to eat him alive. He stopped answering his phone and barely touched his computer.

Excitement had always been his go to drug when the memories encroached on his sanity, but the adrenaline that usually fueled his life or death adventures had gone missing on this trip. Instead, an emptiness had settled deep inside him and nothing seemed willing to take its place. The years since he'd left home had been one risk-taking event after another. He'd had his fair share of close calls and near death experiences and yet here he hung with nothing more than the breathtaking views to keep him alive. He loved to travel. Especially to the remote unspoiled beauty of the wilderness. Although even that rarely made a dent anymore.

His latest adventure had landed him in the red rock canyons of Moab. He'd followed the tourists in and then went in his own direction with not much more than the camping gear on his bike and a small supply of food and water. His solitary pursuit of something more meaningful and intoxicating had kept him going from place to place for quite some time. But these days something else had become more important than the excitement, he longed to put down roots.

He wanted to go home.

Unfortunately, home wasn't exactly his home anymore and after one disastrous and violent night, he'd agreed with Mason and Tucker that he'd never return. Except even in the land of rock climbers and mountain bikers you still got an occasional internet signal and satellite TV and he'd seen some of the entertainment reports on Tucker and his new lady love. The bastard had left the lake in a big way and took a whole mess of reporters with him. He'd hooked up with a professor who taught BDSM to a bunch of baby faced college kids after getting arrested in an FBI raid at a sex club in Florida. The millionaire and the bad girl professor. It was either the makings for a bad porn movie or Tucker's little head had finally won.

What in the hell were he and Mason thinking? The whole point of this shitty mess of their current lives had come about from doing what was best for the greater good and that meant keeping a low fucking profile and protecting those who couldn't protect themselves.

Levi threw his arm across a gap in the rocks and grasped another boulder before releasing his hold on the previous one. Emotions had a way of fueling his exertion and anger was one of the best motivators when he'd overtaxed his body. Stretched wide he struggled for breath. God, he loved the challenge of pushing his body to the breaking point and then taking it one step further. The pain kept him aware of his surroundings and fueled his desire to continue. He had one last big hurdle to the top and then he could rest. He swung his body right and maneuvered his leg between a ridge in the cliff that held him secure while he reached for ledges large enough for his fingers to grab onto. He hauled himself upward and hiked his hip against the rock.

The rock crumbled under his right hand and he lost his grip. His lower body lost traction and he scrambled for anything to grab that would stop his slide on the face of the rock. With a push of adrenaline fueled strength, well beyond his limits, he hauled himself to the top ridge and collapsed facedown onto the flat rock. He'd done it. Once again he'd proven that when he put his mind to a physical challenge he exceeded even his own expectations.

He rolled onto his back and squinted into the sun. Maybe his expectations weren't high enough. He lived day-to-day and week-to-week with very little to show for it. No real home. No people to call his own. Thanks to some strategic real estate investments over the years, he had the freedom to work when he wanted to and to travel when he didn't. Thanks to his preference for a tent in the middle of nowhere, he'd never had to touch a dime of his father's tainted money and that suited him just fine.

Of course that didn't stop Mason from forwarding him his monthly accounting statements with the same asinine question. *Why aren't you spending any money?* He also insisted on him settling down somewhere, putting down roots. This month the email had also insisted he contact him right away with his whereabouts. Mason the control freak couldn't stand not knowing where he was every minute of every day. Whatever.

Levi thought through this baggage every month. His travels took him from one side of the country to the other and to as many countries as he could think of all in the hopes of finding that one place that he would be happy to call home. Unfortunately, nothing called to him. Except one. The forbidden fruit.

What the hell? If Tucker had chased some BDSM loving woman to Boston in full view of the media maybe it meant things were changing back home. If enough time had passed, they could finally get back to their real lives. A strangled bark of laughter erupted from him. Fat fucking chance. Their real lives were about as real as the fake ones. Life interuptus and all that shit way back when. He swiped the sweat from his face and blew out a rough breath. More than a decade and it all still felt like yesterday.

Heat baked through the sweat and dust covering his clothes and body. He reached up and pushed his fingers through his thick hair. He'd let the hair grow out, he was more than halfway to a full beard and his clothes looked like shit. He loved pushing his body past the point of no return but it was time to find something more fulfilling. He pushed to his feet and walked to the edge of the cliff. The panoramic views from the clouds to the ground should have taken his breath away. Instead the constant ache of emptiness had accompanied him on his climb and it wasn't going away.

He definitely needed a change. After he climbed off this motherfucker first. Taking a deep breath and one last sweeping glance around him, he turned and started down the backside. There was a small and uneven trail he could use for about a half mile before he had to start climbing again. That gave him just enough time to recover some of his strength and focus.

If only navigating the past came that easily. Today was the anniversary of his mother's death. Every year he waited for this day to get easier and it never did. He blamed everything on his father's crazy ass and if he wasn't already dead, Levi would have killed him ten times over by now. Of course some might argue his own behavior bordered on some sort of mental disorder fine line not all that different from his father's. The right motivation could push him either way. Into the darkness or out into the light.

Jesus fuck. When had he become so philosophical and maudlin? He wasn't crazy. He just hadn't found where he belonged. He'd spent the last dozen years looking for something that wasn't out there. If he wanted peace then it was time to go home and get it. One way or another. The demons of the past needed to be put down.

They were waiting for him to return...

TWO

Tori Ford grabbed her purse from the back of the chair where she'd left it and dug through the pockets. "Where the heck are my keys?" She scanned the kitchen counters and the pegs on the wall by the door for the fifth time. "Why are they not where I usually leave them? Hannah, have you seen mommy's keys?"

"No," her daughter's sweet voice answered from the back of the house.

Tori opened drawer after drawer as she moved around the generous work island in her kitchen. The urge to clean up the mess from baking ate at the edges of her consciousness as she searched. She hated to leave her kitchen in disarray but she was about to be late delivering her pies. Tori glanced at the clock and bit back a curse. Hannah didn't need to learn any more bad words from her own mother. That's what public school was for.

She twisted from side to side. "How do keys just disappear?"

At that moment her daughter appeared, her pink and white stuffed bag slung over her shoulder, matching pink sunglasses covering her beautiful eyes and her hand on her hip. Tori's heart lurched as it did every morning when her little girl started her day with a dazzling smile.

"These keys, momma?"

Tori laughed when she saw them dangling from Hannah's small fingers. "Yes, Ms. Smarty Pants. Where'd you find them?"

"In the bathroom. I think you left them in there when you went to go potty."

She choked. Straight from the mouths of babes. Tori shook her head and swiped the keys from her child. "I take it you're ready to go."

"Yes, ma'am. I packed my new bathing suit and my crayons and coloring book just like you asked."

"Good girl. Let mommy load the last of these pies into the back and off we'll go."

Hannah frowned. "I wish we had Elvis pie to take with us."

Tori brushed the mess of curls fighting to get free from the headband Hannah had placed on her head. "I know. You've mentioned that problem a few times now." More like fifty. "I promise after we get back from the lake we'll make so many Elvis pies you'll turn into peanut butter and chocolate. Deal?" She held out her hand.

Hannah slapped her hand. "Deal."

Five minutes later the car was loaded and Tori pulled her cheery yellow Volkswagen Beetle into the easy morning traffic. With school out for the summer, there weren't that many cars on the road this time of day. Commuters into the city were long gone and the tiny downtown area had yet to come to life. The slower pace of life and the small closed community was much of what kept her in the area after Hannah's father had walked away from them. The pull to go somewhere for a fresh start had been strong in the beginning, but ultimately the idea of taking Hannah away from all that she knew seemed wrong. Not to mention Tori's sister might have killed her if she'd moved away.

Once Tori drove beyond the town limits even more of the area's charm took over. Trees and grass were one thing, but the lake never failed to take her breath away. She was drawn to the water in a way she didn't totally understand. Unable to afford even a small house this close to the water she'd taken the second best option of a tiny house in town with the option of both residential and commercial zoning. With a little hard work and a lot more money she could turn the extra building next to her home into a small pie shop.

Minutes later, she pulled into the parking lot of Nina's cafe. She whipped around to the back of the building and backed her small car into the spot closest to the kitchen door. Tori grabbed her purse and keys and then entered the cafe with Hannah hot on her heels. There were a few customers scattered inside in various stages of breakfast so Tori steered her daughter toward the empty counter.

"Why don't you get out your crayons and sit here for a minute while I help Miss Nina get the pies into the back. Then as soon as we do, you and I will be headed to the lake for a swim. Sound good?"

Her daughter nodded and climbed onto the stool at the end of the counter next to the pie case. "If someone comes in for pie can I get it for them? I'm a big girl now."

Tori laid out Hannah's coloring book and a few crayons. "No, young lady, you may not. We won't be gone long and if someone new comes in I'm sure they won't mind waiting a few minutes for us to return."

"But, Momma I--"

"Nope. Coloring, Hannah. That's it."

Her daughter's exasperated sigh made her want to laugh out loud. Precocious didn't even begin to describe her child. It seemed from the day she'd learned to walk and talk she'd been on. Now she was five going on sixteen.

Tori pushed through the kitchen door and went in search of Nina. When she didn't see her in the kitchen she opted for the small office in the back. As she neared the door she heard Nina talking.

"C'mon, Tucker. Stop being a pussy."

Tori paused mid step, her jaw dropping open. Nina was apparently on the phone with her brother and if there was anything she'd learned since befriending the woman it was how much she loved to razz her brother. They often went at it like teenagers and with very colorful language. Now that he'd left to stay with his girlfriend on her temporary assignment up north, she'd been antsy for his return.

"Yeah, yeah. Whatever. You are full of excuses. As far as I'm concerned you need to get it over with and get your ass back down here."

Tori couldn't decide whether to knock or head back to the dining room. She didn't want to spy on a private conversation.

"No, most of them have gone now. Except that one. In fact I heard she's moved from her hotel to a small apartment. I don't think she's going away."

Silence ensued as Tori imagined Nina listening to Tucker on the other end. She didn't have a clue what was going on but Nina had talked to her at great length about the unusual reunion of her brother with Maggie. A high school friend who'd come back to town amidst a sex scandal that had made national news. For a few weeks there had been reporters bugging Nina trying to get her to talk about Tucker.

"Yeah. Mason says he handling her but he's acting stranger than ever. I'm ready to gouge his eyes out if he doesn't stop hovering over every little thing I do."

Another pause.

"Of course I'm not dating. Can you imagine the hell Mason would create? The overbearing assh--"

Tori stifled a giggle. She'd seen Mason and Nina bicker on more than one occasion and she didn't get it. For a while she'd thought they had a thing for each other until Nina had set her straight on that nonsense as she'd so delicately put it but with stronger words. Unwilling to stand here and eavesdrop on the conversation any longer, Tori stepped forward and knocked on the door.

The door opened and Nina motioned her inside. "Anyways... Tori is here and some of us actually have to work for a living."

Tori couldn't hear Tucker's response but she could easily imagine it as Nina stuck out her tongue and rolled her eyes.

"I'll believe it when I see it. In the meantime find your balls and get it done so you two can come back home. I miss you."

She turned her back to Nina and grinned at the wall behind her. Mouth and all, it was so damned obvious how much Nina cared for her brother.

"Call me after and tell me how it went."

Another pause.

"Oh my God. Ewwww. I do not want to hear about your weird sex life. I'm hanging up now. Bye." She placed the old-fashioned phone receiver into its cradle on her desk. "I don't understand why he insists on reminding me about his kinky lifestyle. Yuck. Who wants to be reminded that their brother likes to tie up women and... Just yuck."

Tori laughed. "You're just offended because he's your brother. If I confessed to a sex life that included whips and chains you'd press me for every last detail."

Nina hopped off her desk and stalked toward Tori. "Are you holding out on me? Have you met someone? Oh my God I'm going to kill you if you're sleeping with someone I don't know about."

Tori held up her hands to stop Nina's tirade. "Whoa there, nutso. I didn't mean that literally. It was very much a what if scenario. Not only do I not have the desire or time for a man, do you honestly think Hannah is ready for something like that?" She shook her head and tried to get the idea out of her mind.

"How long has it been? Almost two years? I'd say you were overdue. And it's possible to have a sex life that your kid doesn't know about. Come on, you act like an old woman sometimes."

"Hello kettle, meet pot. Last I checked you haven't been out on a date in," she paused for effect. "In forever."

Nina's face changed. The intensity and humor of moments before disappeared. For a second Tori got the idea that there was something going on in her friend's head that she wasn't sharing. Moments later, it was gone.

"Did you bring me some good pies today? The natives are getting restless for more."

Tori's face heated. She still wasn't used to the many compliments that had been pouring in over her desserts. It had given her renewed hope that a pie shop might be a good idea after all. "Yep, I've got four kinds out in the car. I came to grab you to help me unload them."

"Awesome, then let's get to it." Nina headed to the door and Tori followed her. Before they made it through the door her friend turned and stared her down. "Don't think this conversation is over yet, Ms. Ford. I've got my eye on you now and if you aren't having sex, then it's high time we find you someone."

Tori stood frozen to the spot as Nina sashayed out of the room. Just great. Now she'd have Suzy matchmaker on her butt bugging her to get laid.

"Hey, don't go getting any ideas," she hollered to her friend as she followed her out the back door. "Two can definitely play that game."

THREE

Levi drove to the lake on his way into town. He watched the sun rising over the water and waited for the area around him to come alive. People arrived to launch boats and women brought their small children to play in the lakeside park. The low buzz of small town life wrapped around him like a warm towel straight out of the dryer. How long had it been since he'd felt something so simple and comforting? The morning hours passed by in quiet slow motion until the heat settled in and Levi decided it was time to move on to the next step.

First stop, for lack of a better idea on where to go he drove straight to the one place he expected to find the least amount of grief.

His ass hurt and he was starving. Three full days and half nights on his bike crossing from Utah to North Carolina had been a whirlwind. Once he'd made up his mind to go home no amount of scenery or call of adventure could sway him from his mission. When he'd finally hit the county limits, he'd skirted the town and headed straight out here. He rounded the final curve and slowed the beast underneath him.

The small cafe looked exactly like he'd remembered it.

A simple building that had been painted red probably more times than he could count with a traditional southern porch spanning the length of the entire place. There were rocking chairs placed out front that encouraged people to stop and rest or to sit and chat. At the moment there was no one standing outside and only a few cars in the parking lot. He'd managed to hit the slow part of the day. Thank God. He wasn't quite ready to take on the full small town welcome and gossip mill. That would come soon enough. Maybe after he finally got a shave and a shower. He didn't want to think about how he must smell.

He pulled around back and parked alongside a familiar blue pick up. Seriously? In twelve years Nina had never bothered to upgrade? He was surprised that Mason hadn't shoved all kinds of new shit down her throat by now. He set the kickstand and slid off the bike. His bones popped and creaked and he unfolded to his full height in slow motion. Yep, he'd been sitting too damned long.

His bike was loaded down with basic travel gear and the few meager belongings he'd thought worthy of bringing. Not that he had to worry about them out here. This wasn't the city and the odds of anyone touching the junk he carried were about slim to none.

He brushed some of the dust from his jeans and tried to straighten his too wrinkled t-shirt. Not that it helped. He was covered in road crud and nothing short of a washing machine would help. With a shrug, he gave in to the urge to go inside and walked away from his bike. At the front door he took a deep breath and prepared himself for the coming storm Nina.

He stepped inside and welcomed the cool air conditioning on his burned skin. He'd given a fleeting thought to sunscreen a few states back and had never bothered to stop. Now that the road wind had disappeared, the hot and humid Carolina summer heat hit him full force.

He welcomed the change in temperature and took a few slow breaths to adjust. In doing so it dawned on him he'd not been immediately tackled. In fact, there was stone cold silence surrounding him. Except...

At the far end of the counter a small girl sat on a stool scribbling on some paper in front of her. She turned his way and smiled, a big adorable grin not worthy of some stranger like him. A cloud of black curly hair surrounded her face and fell to her shoulders. She brushed a few strands out of her eyes and blew on the rest. "Come on in. My momma said if anyone came in while she was in back I should tell you to get a menu at the register and pick a seat anywhere. She's coming right back."

Her momma? Holy shit. Nina had a child and no one had seen fit to inform him? He felt a little weak in the knees. He grabbed the edge of the counter and steadied himself. Did that mean he had a—

"If you don't want to sit by yourself, you can sit next to me. I've got extra crayons and I don't mind sharing."

Levi was taken aback by the adorable child offering to share her crayons with him. He'd never gotten much of a chance to spend time with any kids and yet this one made him curious. He grabbed one of the menus at the cashier and then walked to the end of the counter where she sat watching him with an innocent curiosity that pulled at him. Why the hell she wasn't calling for her mother or running away as fast as she could shocked him. He didn't need a mirror to know how rough he looked. To a child, he'd be downright scary.

"I'd be honored to share your crayons." He slid onto the stool next to her and took the offered piece of paper she now held in her hand and placed it on the counter. He glanced at her paper. "What are you drawing?"

She picked up a green crayon and scribbled furiously across the bottom of her picture. "My house," she replied.

"You live near here?"

"Uh huh. Me and Momma just stopped here on our way to the lake. She promised to take me swimming after she delivered new pies to Miss Nina. Miss Nina loves my momma's pies. She's got cherry, and apple and peach and everyone's favorite Dewberry."

Levi stopped drawing and stared at the little girl. "Did you say your mom brought pies?"

"Yeah, do you like pie? I love pie. I like the Elvis pie the best cause its got chocolate and peanut butter, but my momma didn't make any of those today. That makes me sad. Oh and my name's Hannah by the way. What's yours?"

His head spun from the little girl's rambling. She'd just given him a mouthful of information and all he could think about was the pie. Whoever her mother was, she made pie. "My name is Levi and I love pie. In fact I'm starving and I think I'll have to just order pie. Maybe one slice of each."

The little girl giggled. A sweet sound that made it impossible for Levi not to smile, however foreign the sensation.

"You can't just have pie. That's cheating. You have to eat your lunch first. My momma says so, Mr. Levi."

"Your momma sounds like a smart lady."

"Oh she is. She's saving up so we can have our own pie store. Right here." The little girl pointed to a small building next to the house she'd drawn. "She said I can work there with her and we'll get to make pies every day. Making pie is fun. Have you ever made a pie?"

"What about school. Don't you go?"

"Not yet." She put down the green crayon and picked up a blue one and began drawing fluffy clouds. "I start when the summer is over. I'm going to be in kindergarten. I'm five now."

Levi soaked in everything she told him while creating his own drawing. He couldn't ever remember using crayons before today, although he must have at some point in his childhood. Obviously this child saw the moon and the stars in her mother, as she should. For a moment he thought of his own mother and the way she used to take care of him. A sharp stab of pain nearly sliced him in two. He slammed that door shut and forced his brain to think of other things. Better not to go there.

"You sure have a lot of tattoos. These right here remind me of momma's tattoos." She pointed to his right forearm and made a large circle around one section. "Except hers aren't on her arm. They cover her private parts."

Holy shit! Levi went light headed at the thought. All of a sudden he really wanted to meet this child's mother. If she was half as intriguing as her little girl...

Thinking about everything Hannah had said so far he realized she'd made no mention of a father. Yes, he definitely looked forward to finding out who this child belonged to. The fact she baked pies was enough for him. But a woman with tattoos on her private parts? That made his head swim.

Wonder if she'll marry me?

"Wow. Five. Such a great age. You'll be grown up and living on your own before you know it."

Hannah laughed. "Oh no. I'm never leaving momma alone. That would make her too sad. Like when daddy left."

Bingo. A missing father. That explained a lot.

"Hannah. What are you doing?"

The sound of a woman's voice joining their conversation startled Levi. Had to be the now infamous mother. He glanced in the direction of the mystery woman and felt his mouth go dry.

Standing before him was an older, more exotic version of the little girl sitting to his right. The same cloud of curly dark hair surrounded her face and fell halfway down her arms, one side pushed behind an ear as if in a futile effort to

23

control it. Round face with very tanned skin. Eyes a little too wide set, but the color of rich, dark chocolate. Of course, the full ruby red lips currently pursed in a frown in his direction only enhanced the look. Maybe not classically beautiful, but mesmerizing nonetheless. The long elegant line of her bare neck drew his gaze. She had the perfect throat for his hand--or a collar. As much as he wanted to check out the rest of the package he forced his gaze to return to hers without going any further south than her throat.

"Momma!" the girl squealed. "This is Levi and he's coloring with me and he wants pie. Can he have pie before he eats lunch? Cause I told him that was cheating."

The woman's face transformed to a soft genuine smile when she turned to look at her daughter. "I think as long as his mother isn't here to tell him that he can't have pie, then one piece before lunch won't hurt. Grown-ups have different rules from chatty little girls. You should start cleaning up your mess, Hannah. As soon as Ms. Nina comes in from out back we'll be leaving."

For a second the little girl looked at him with the saddest eyes he'd ever seen. That was something he couldn't bear from someone so young and innocent. He wanted to reach out and give her a hug. Of course he imagined her mother bear would have a thing or two to say about some dirty, tattooed biker touching her little girl.

"Yes, momma," she finally replied. "I'm sorry I can't stay longer and color with you so you don't have to eat your pie alone, Mr. Levi."

He swallowed against the sad gaze she fixed on him. Lord help him, if he wasn't careful he'd soon be a puddle of mush on the floor at the hands of this one. "Hannah, don't worry about me darlin'. If your momma's pie is even half as good as you say it is, I'm sure we'll see each other again." The little girl gave him a sweet smile.

"So, Levi was it? If you don't want to wait for Nina to come back in, I could get you a slice. Did you know what flavor you want?"

Levi's body tightened when his name rolled off her tongue in a soft southern accent. She needed to say that again. Maybe over and over again. He thought about telling her he could wait but he wasn't quite ready to end his conversation with Hannah's mother. In fact, when she leaned across the counter to help her daughter with her crayons he got a whiff of something that made his eyes cross. Woman and sugar spun together in a heady mix. For a split second he imagined that lush scent mingled with the darker undertone of sex...

Shit, he needed to get his head out of his pants. Thank God the counter hid his visceral reaction.

"I think your lovely daughter mentioned peach. Peach pie is my favorite." At least what he really wanted didn't come tumbling out of his mouth. She'd run screaming if she saw inside his head. If Hannah wasn't here he'd be tempted to ask for a slice of her. Right here on this counter so he could lick her from head to toe and back again. He wanted a taste of her.

And there were the tattoos he now needed to discover...

"Sure. No problem."

"I told him Elvis pie was my favorite but that you didn't make any of that today." Hannah followed her statement with the cutest little pout.

"You are incorrigible, young lady. I already promised you after we get back from the lake you can help me make Elvis pie. But if you don't slow down on eating it all we'll have to start calling it Fat Elvis Pie. Now go change into your suit, but remember to put the shorts on over it and the flip flops back on your feet. We still have to walk down there." She pinched Hannah's cheek and turned toward the pie case.

Hannah leaned close and lowered her voice. "She doesn't really mean that. She always tells me I'm as skinny as a bean pole." At that she scooted in the direction of the restroom while sing songing about the lake, taking a little piece of his heart with her. He turned back and came face to face with the most gorgeous ass clad in denim he'd ever seen bent over in front of him. After a stunned moment he had to roll his tongue back into his mouth and lift his chin off the counter.

"I hope you like vanilla ice cream with your pie. I took the liberty of adding a scoop." She turned around and slid the plate in front of him. For the first time in well, ever he'd found something he wanted more than peach pie.

"You've got a great little girl there."

"She's precocious and trusting."

She'd been eyeballing him with caution since she'd come through the kitchen door and now that Hannah had left the room, the easygoing mother had disappeared with her. "And you're not? Trusting that is?"

"I'm cautious. Strangers tend to stick out around here. It being a small town and all."

"Fair enough." Levi scooped his first bite of this woman's peach pie into his mouth and the taste bud explosion nearly melted him into the stool. "Holy shit. This is sooo good."

Some of the starch holding her back ramrod straight began to soften and a sweet looking smile transformed her face into that of a spectacular beauty. He felt his tongue tying itself into knots. "I'm glad you like--"

"Oh. My. God. Levi?"

They both turned at the intrusion and found a shocked Nina standing at the kitchen door. Jeans, t-shirt and a massive amount of blonde hair stood all of about five foot two in front of them. Considering she looked almost exactly as he'd last seen her, he'd guess she loved her life here. He'd always wondered why she never left. Out of all of them she had the most reasons for wanting to get the hell out of this town. How else would she put the past behind her?

Nina's secrets weren't all secrets around these parts. He didn't remember the details, but her mother's affair with Tucker's father had become well known gossip for a while. It wasn't until she turned eighteen that things got really ugly. Levi tried to tamp down the dark thoughts that plagued him. How one tiny night could alter so many lives and for so long struck him as the biggest injustice of it all. How did she put it behind her when he never had?

"Is that you under all that hair and grime? Good Lord did you forget how to use soap?" She took a few steps closer. "I saw a strange bike out back and came to check it out. Did you join a biker gang or something? Is that the reason for this?" She waved her arms up and down in front of him.

He grinned and took another huge bite of the amazing pie. Nina was just getting started and knowing her she'd have a lot to say. From the corner of his eye he watched Hannah's mother move away from him. Shit. He hadn't even asked her for her name yet.

"It's nice to see you too, Nina."

"I'd give you a hug but I think I'd have to take you out back and hose you off first. And I don't even want to know how you smell."

"That's okay I'd rather finish this amazing pie first. Good God this is incredible."

Nina looked between him and Hannah's mother and narrowed her eyes ever so slightly. After an awkward silence of several long seconds she finally spoke again, "I take it you met, Tori."

Tori. Hmm. Not the name he would have imagined for such an incredible beauty. She needed a name that matched.

Tori and Hannah. He mulled the names in his head for a moment. What a combo. "Actually it was Hannah who greeted me first when I walked through the door. She's the one who sold me on her mother's pie."

Just like Tori, Nina's face transformed at the mention of the little girl. "Oh isn't she a sweetie? I keep offering to take her off Tori's hands and for some reason she remains attached."

Tori laughed. "Nina you are as incorrigible as Hannah."

"If that's all I am then I must be off my game today. I'll have to try harder." She turned back to Levi. "Now, what do I owe the honor of this visit after all these years? Where have you been all this time? Does Mason know you're here? Did I miss his reaction? Shit. That would have been priceless."

Levi took the last bite and savored it, letting Nina's questions linger. Maybe when he figured out where he'd be staying tonight, Tori would sell him a whole pie. He put down his fork and pushed the empty plate away from him. "To answer your questions. I was ready to come home, you name it I've been there and no, Mason does not know I'm here and I really don't care."

Nina let go a low loud whistle. "He's going to shit a brick when he finds out. You know how much he hates surprises."

"That's his problem. It's been over a decade since I left and the time has come for change, I'm not leaving again."

Nina cocked her head. "That's quite an ultimatum. I hope you're ready for the fallout. She shrugged, not waiting for him to respond. "You heard about Tucker and Maggie then." She shook her head. "What am I saying, of course you did. Everyone in the free world and beyond has heard about those two."

"Yeah what is that about? We go from total silence to--"

"Look, Mr. Levi, I'm ready to go to the lake!" Hannah's excited voice broke through the conversation he'd been having with Nina while totally forgetting they weren't alone anymore.

"Wow. Don't you look beautiful, sweetheart. You'll be the star at the lake today." To his surprise, she literally beamed at his words. He also didn't miss the strange look that Nina gave him. Fortunately Tori rescued the growing tension by scooping up Hannah's bags and corralling her toward the door.

"Nina, I'll see you in a couple of days. You should be set until then but if you need anything before then just give me a call. We're making a fresh batch of the Elvis pies if you want some."

Nina waved the other woman off. "Don't worry about a thing. Unless Levi here eats half the inventory I should be good to go. This scary, hairy big lug has a true obsession with pie."

Both women laughed as Tori and Hannah slipped out the front door. When they'd disappeared from sight, Levi took a slow breath and blew it out. He had a lot to think about tonight. Moments after the door closed it reopened and an adorable flash of dark hair and pink swimsuit came running through.

"Mr. Levi thank you for meeting me today. I think you should keep this to remember me by."

Levi knelt down and took the offered paper from Hannah's hands. It was the drawing of her house and the pie shop she'd been working on when he sat down with her. "Aww, sweetheart you don't have to give me this. You worked so hard on it. I bet your mother would love it."

"I really want you to have it. Please."

He couldn't tear his gaze from the almost pleading look in her eyes. "Of course, Hannah. I'd love to keep it and I'll treasure it."

Her smile widened and he noticed that just like her mother, her beauty transformed. When her little one grew up, Tori would have to beat off all the teenage boys who would darken her doorstep.

His chest tightened as Hannah spun on her flower topped flip-flops and flew out the door and into the parking lot where her mother waited. For a few seconds he locked gazes with Tori and he didn't know what to think. There was an aura of sadness and distrust surrounding her as she kept an eagle eye on her child. It made a strange pang in his chest when he thought about wiping that look permanently from her face. With only his instincts to go on, he contemplated there was a whole lot more to Tori and Hannah than met the eye. Then they were both gone and silence ensued.

"That's a really bad idea, Levi," Nina warned. "Tori has had it real rough for a long time. She needs to find a nice quiet man with no drama. She absolutely cannot handle someone like you."

"Someone like me? Wow, way to be a bi--"

"If you finish that sentence like that you'll get an up close and personal lesson with my little pink stun gun. And then maybe when you're twitching on the ground unable to put a coherent word together you'll think about what comes out of your mouth."

"You don't think in a decade plus I might have changed? Grown up a little?"

Nina looked him up and down. "Not that much. Seriously, have you looked in a mirror lately? I'm surprised both Hannah and Tori didn't run from the café in fear."

He was too.

"Why would you want to come back here anyway? Where ever you were has got to be better for you than here."

Nina's surly attitude shocked him. He didn't know why,

but he'd thought she might not mind seeing him again. Some of the hopelessness he'd been trying to fight came back stronger than before. "This is the only home I have and I intend to stay." He waited a few heartbeats, hoping for a response. None came and the weight of more disappointment added to the thick layers around his heart. "I just wanted to come home again."

FOUR

Levi poked at the wood burning in the fire pit and stoked the flame higher. After Nina's disappointing reaction he'd left the cafe and headed straight here to the house he'd grown up in. If her reaction was any indication, he'd be starting over on his own. This would be the place to do it. The small home on Cherry Street outside the city limits of Davidson had been left exactly as he remembered. He hadn't bothered to have the electricity turned on before he arrived so he'd be roughing it for a few days. A little digging in the old shed had netted him the special wrench he'd crafted as a teenager, which allowed him to turn on the water whenever they got disconnected for failure to pay. Those were the days.

The first thing he'd done was clean the one bathroom and take a shower. The clothes he'd worn into town, along with a heap of junk from inside the house, now sat in the middle of the fire pit burning away. Levi lifted the tequila bottle he'd brought outside with him and took a swig. The bitter alcohol burned like the lowest ring of hell going down. Jesus hell. The rot gut he'd found in the kitchen cabinet had to be the nastiest liquor he'd ever tasted. Unwilling to take another sip of the foul shit, Levi poured the rest into the fire and watched the flames jump wildly. At least it was good for something.

He stared into the orange glow and wondered if coming back here had been the best idea. Nina was right. There were a lot of bad memories here. Ones that no matter how hard he tried, never really went away. They weren't all bad though. He picked up the photo album he'd uncovered in one of the living room cabinets and opened it to the first page. His baby photo greeted him. He'd been born red faced, skinny and with a head full of jet-black hair. He also found the hospital card with his birth stats and another piece of paper with his footprints. Father had been left blank and for so long he'd not known why. Then he'd learned the hard way there had been a very good reason. Blinking the bad away, he focused on what came before *that* night.

She'd been a great mother. As far as he could tell she'd saved every important paper and documented every milestone of his entire childhood in this book. For nearly twenty years she'd played both mother and father. He slammed the book shut and tossed it back on the nearby patio table. He still couldn't think of her without thinking of *him*.

This wasn't the way to spend his first night back home. He should be out enjoying the night and having a good time. The point had been to quit spending all his time alone with nature and bad memories. But where? After all this time he didn't know if anyone he knew from high school still lived in the area and he didn't have a clue how much had changed.

There was one place he could go.

Mason would have a conniption, but better to get the confrontation with his friend over with. He'd just have to get used to the fact that he'd come back to live here now. Tomorrow he'd start gutting his mother's house and turn it into something else. A place more suited to him, where he

LEVI'S ULTIMATUM

could make his own memories. When he sat down to sketch some of it out he'd considered selling and moving closer to the lake and quickly changed his mind. The house wasn't much but the land gave him more than enough room and this far outside any city limits there wasn't a lot of oversight as to what he could and couldn't do out here. Not to mention it made a great place to start a family.

That made him think of the little girl he'd met today. And her mother... He envied that bond.

So he'd renovate instead of selling and buying new. Fortunately, over the years he'd picked up a few skills here and there when he needed to save some money in the early days of his real estate investments. What he couldn't handle on his own he'd hire out. Living out of a pack on the back of a motorcycle off and on for the last several years had given him one benefit. He'd managed to save a lot of his own money. Clean money that he'd earned and wasn't tainted by his father.

Shit. Memory lane would not leave him alone.

Maybe a good scene at the club was a better idea than he'd thought. He could wipe away some of the lingering memories he couldn't shake tonight.

Levi sat back down in the chair and watched the fire until it dwindled to nothing but warm embers. Thinking about Purgatory made him think about the primal reaction he'd had to Tori earlier in the day. Something buried so deep inside him had awakened and apparently had no intention of letting up. The rest of the day, random images of her in different types of bondage kept popping in his head at random times. There was probably a special kind of hell for him to be having thoughts like that after spending time with her child. She was a busy mother who had barely given him the time of day. She'd more likely give him a piece of her mind and a lecture about staying away from her than she'd let him restrain her.

35

Levi sighed. He had to do something to get the damned woman off his mind. Resigned to going out and mingling with some fresh faces he strode into the house and hunted out his keys. He found them on the kitchen counter sitting on top of a very important piece of paper. The drawing Hannah had gifted him before she'd run off with her mother. For a split second he thought about going to see Tori instead of heading to the club. She'd have more pie. Maybe she'd show him her tattoos… Then he glanced at the clock and decided against it. Nothing looked more stalkerish than showing up at someone's home at eleven o'clock at night with the only excuse being he needed more pie. It'd be almost worth it just for the pie if it didn't sound so damned pathetic.

So he carried the drawing over to the refrigerator and stuck it on the door with some of the old magnets still hanging around. Even though it was a crude child's drawing, there was something familiar about the two buildings that he couldn't quite place. He shrugged. Maybe it would hit him later. He scooped up his keys and headed out the door. Time to face the music.

Levi circled the block three times before he found a parking place. In some vague spot in his memory he'd known that Purgatory had grown into a huge success but damn. This was a hell of a lot more than he'd expected. He approached the front door through the throngs of people waiting to get in and flashed his ID to the woman working the door.

"I'm sorry, Sir. But we have a bit of a wait tonight. If you want to wait in line I'll get you in as fast as I can," she offered.

"Did you check the VIP list?"

She lifted her brows and took him in. Jeans, black t-shirt and beat up cowboy boots. Probably not the typical attire worn in the club, but if they now had some sort of dress code bullshit for Doms he'd have to kick someone's ass. Change was one thing, pretentious something or other entirely different. Levi stood still and allowed her silent questions to linger between them. He had no intention of offering any other information but he understood her reluctance when it came to a stranger. In fact, it made her an employee worth noting.

Finally she handed back his drivers license and nodded toward the lobby behind her. "The elevator to the VIP section is to the right when you enter the door. Welcome to the Purgatory Club, Sir."

"Thanks, darlin," he winked at the lovely woman and proceeded inside. The shiny brass elevators he found were certainly new. Someone had made some major upgrades while he'd been gone. He rode to the second floor and savored the complete silence that would soon end. In all honesty, he'd had more than his fair share of silence over the years. He was good and ready for some excitement.

The bell dinged and the doors slid open. Immediately his ears were assaulted by the sound of blaring techno music these types of clubs favored. Every city had one whether they knew it or not. It was a little cliché, but it was damned hard to break some traditions. He made his way through the narrow balcony that led to the main second floor play space. Fortunately, the music was not the focus here in Purgatory, it simply provided the ambiance. Below he could see throngs of Goth partiers on the dance floor surrounded by two stages that currently had live dancers performing. This wasn't a strip club and full nudity wasn't allowed in the public spaces, so the dancers were clothed in various forms of leather, vinyl and fur. With the fake smoke and the light show he couldn't make out any further details from the first floor.

He proceeded towards the back of the room and

the fully stocked bar. The balcony wrapped the entire building, making it the perfect vantage point to all the general activities going on below as well as the ability to observe all of the play stations set up on this floor. In one of Mason's many reports he'd learned the cost of admission to the VIP section came at a much higher price, but it gave anyone willing to pay a deeper look into the fetish scenes going on around them within limits. The third floor, however, was an entirely different story. Members only and by invitation only. There he'd find a submissive willing to play with him who would understand all of his needs without having to go home with him to be happy.

It was hard to believe that the place he stood in now had started out as a fraternity for he, Tucker and Mason when they'd discovered they all shared similar sexual tastes. They'd been kinky fuckers even back then. Their lives had snowballed from that one decision and fate had been a cruel bitch to them all.

Jesus H. Fuck that. He needed to stop obsessing over the past.

He stopped in front of a cute bartender with long brown hair that looked like it would be silky to the touch. He had a thing for women's hair. Especially when it was clenched in his hand as she came so hard on his dick she thought she'd die. Fortunately or unfortunately for this one, depending on how he looked at it, she wore a thick red and orange flame-shaped collar at her neck. Already owned.

"What can I get you, Sir?" she asked. She looked straight in his eyes when she asked and then quickly cast her gaze down. It amazed him how easily trained submissives could spot a Dominant so quickly. It was a lovely skill that he hadn't seen in a very long time.

"Tequila shot."

"Do you have a preference on brand or just house?" she asked.

He shook his head. "House'll do." He watched her hands move fast and efficient while she carried out her task. She'd been doing this a while. He wanted to learn more about the inner workings of Purgatory and maybe talking to the bartender would yield something interesting.

"Would you--"

"Hey, Ruby!" The guy at the other end of the bar hollered down at her and shook the phone he was holding in his hand. "Zane's on the phone." He watched her features soften at the mention of the caller. Her Dom, he'd bet.

"Sorry, if you need anything else just let Dave know and he'll get it."

He nodded and watched her go. His curiosity piqued to know more, he gestured to the other bartender. As a self-confessed people watcher and part owner of this club, it felt weird to be the stranger here.

"I didn't get to give her a tip before she ran off." He handed the bartender a large bill and he accepted it.

"Oh I'm sure she doesn't mind. With her Dom on the phone she tends to forget everything else," the man admitted.

"Sounds like she's a good girl then."

The man snickered. "I don't think I'd ever call Ruby a good girl to her face and think for a second I'd get away with it. Our little firebug has a temper and if your name ain't Zane or Gabe she isn't likely to listen to a word you say."

Gabe. Now there was a name he remembered all too well. He'd been as close to a fourth in their tight knit group as possible without being related by blood. "Do you mean Gabe Michaels? Is that old dog still around here?" He knew he was but might as well play it up for this guy. They'd all played this game for so long it came as second nature now. Made it easier to keep their business secret. Which made him think of Tucker. Just how much had Tucker revealed to his new lady professor? And what about all the reporters? Was Mason even bothering with damage control anymore?

"Yep, that's him. Sounds like you know the manager." Levi didn't love the strong hint of curiosity coming from the bartender. Time to move on.

"Yeah. I knew him once. A long time ago. Maybe I'll look him up again." With that he pushed away from the bar and headed for the largest crowd. He'd disappear from sight and the bartender would forget all about him. As he approached the space he heard the distinct sound of a flogger hitting bare flesh. For a minute he allowed his eyes to slide closed and let the sound carry him away. It had been so long since he'd heard it and it had a way of making his blood zing.

From the sound of the groans coming from the other side of the crowd he guessed a male submissive had taken the cross. From his vantage point he should have been able to see more but a few really tall people in the front were crowding the space. He leaned to the left and made out the man shackled face down on the cross but the person wielding the flogger eluded him. He or she was still hidden by the crowd.

Determined to get closer, he shouldered his way through the crowd with surprising ease. When he finally got to the viewing area he stopped short at the sight of the lovely Domme in charge of the scene. Dressed in a black vinyl bustier that reflected every speck of light in the club and bounced it through the room, a ridiculously short skirt that showed as much of her ass as it covered and thigh high black patent boots that made her legs look like they'd go on forever. But it was her hair that really caught his eye and grabbed a hold of his balls.

Long, well past the middle of her back and every inch of it wild and curly. At the moment she had her back to him and he soaked in the view to the fullest extent. Levi didn't switch ever but the way this woman moved made him wonder what she'd feel like pressed against his back. Or better yet his front pressed to the delectable curve of her generous ass. He bit back a groan at the thought. She swung her arm and he got his first glimpse of her profile. She wore a small black mask across her eyes, which enhanced a strong nose and bright red lips. He normally didn't love a woman's face with that much make up on but she knew how to apply it in a way that only enhanced the glorious look of her olive complexion.

Dark skin, wild long hair and an ass so full he ached to have a handful. Too bad she was a...

She turned again and he got a better glimpse. *Fuck.* Alarm bells went off in his mind. Wait a good god damned minute. No way. He jostled position with the man next to him so he could get a better look at her face and swore when he did, the blood had to have drained from his face.

This wasn't just some Club Domme working the crowd. Masked be damned, he was staring into the face of the woman he'd met this morning at the café. The one whose image had been burned into his brain all damned day. This was Hannah's mother.

Tori.

Shock and anger pushed through his system. He barely stopped himself from barging into the scene and demanding to know what the hell she was doing in his club. The danger in interrupting a scene, not to mention being a complete jackass stopped him. Barely. These people didn't know him from Adam so starting something now would only make things worse.

That didn't mean he was leaving either. He crossed his arms over his chest and refused to take his eyes off of her. The idea of her as a Domme had never even occurred to him. Not for a second. Sure she'd given off an aura of badass mother bear around Hannah, but any woman would protect her children against a stranger, especially one who'd looked like he had.

She flicked her wrist again and the falls of her flogger went flying through the air to land once again on the man's bare back. Angry red streaks covered every bit of naked skin he had visible and he imagined what was hidden under the pants would show marks as well. He turned back to Tori and found her staring at him. Their gazes met and he knew right away she recognized him despite the changes in his appearance. He'd opted to keep the beard after cutting a few inches off. However, the tattoos covering both arms were a dead giveaway.

Behind her little cat mask, her eyes went wide and her mouth dropped open. Damned hot look if he said so himself. He raised his right eyebrow and gave her the look that had cowed many an opponent. To her credit, she smirked in return and turned away from him. She moved back into position and threw another hard lash across the man's back. To everyone else in the room she looked perfectly in control, but he had an eye for the tiniest detail at any distance and this close it was easy to see her hand tremble.

Tori moved to her table and exchanged the flogger for a small soft towel. She handed it to the sub's companion and provided the necessary instructions for ending the scene. The woman moved to the cross and began the task of soothing her submissive and cleaning the station.

He couldn't take his eyes off Tori. Every move, every look, he wanted to absorb it all. With her back to him as she cleaned her workstation, he found himself studying her amazing curves once again. The more he watched her the less he understood the Domme thing. It didn't fit. The passion had been missing from her eyes. Her face wasn't flushed. Now he did have to talk to Gabe. If she worked at the club as a pro Domme he'd know better than anyone the real deal.

In the meantime, he had an idea.

She turned to the crowd. "Who's next?"

"I am," Levi answered.

Another man shouldered next to him. "Nope, sorry. I'm next on the sign up sheet."

Levi stared at the man, ready to do whatever it took to take the next spot on her cross.

"Actually, boys, Cat is going on a break."

Levi turned to the familiar voice and found his old friend Gabe standing directly behind Tori. Wait. Did he call her Cat? Before he could get a question out the man standing next to him started to shake.

"But I've been waiting for over an hour for my turn with Mistress Cat." His voice trembled and Levi half expected him to break out in tears.

"Sorry, Daniel. Don't worry, Mistress Lisa will work you over just as well tonight, I promise." A buxom blonde dressed in a tight leather cat suit stepped out from behind Gabe and took Daniel's hand. She led him to the small altar against the wall and placed him on his knees with his nose pressed to the floor. Levi neither heard what the Domme said or really cared. He'd already turned his attention back to Tori.

"What are *you* doing here?" She fired her question at him, taking him by surprise. Her tone did not carry even a remote shred of the kind woman who'd given him the best peach pie earlier in the day. She sounded angry but her eyes looked scared.

Only a sharp look from Gabe caught him from blurting out that he owned this club and had the right to do whatever the hell he wanted to. Shit. How had twenty minutes in her presence thrown him this off balance?

"Someone might ask you the same thing. You don't belong here," he asserted.

Her eyes widened and several onlookers in the crowd gasped.

"Why don't we take this to my office. I think the crowd has seen enough of a show for one night." Gabe didn't wait for a response. He simply turned and walked away with the full expectation of someone in his position that his wishes would be followed.

Tori shot Levi one last glare before she spun and followed. Levi leaned against the post and crossed his arms. Fuck that. Being led around the club by another Dom wasn't the first impression he planned to make in his own damn place. After a few minutes, when it became apparent he wasn't moving, the normal activities around him resumed and he pretended to watch. When the scene in front of him grew intense and the crowd got completely consumed by the show, Levi did a quick lap around the second floor before proceeding down the stairs to the much more crowded first floor.

He passed by the closed door of the club manager's office and made his way to the back stairs. Pissing matches were not his style and he wouldn't engage now. Not to mention the black mood encroaching wouldn't bode well for Tori if he spoke to her now. He'd either throttle her or fuck her and then where would they be?

He stopped by the lower level bar and grabbed a bottle of tequila. He didn't want to leave, but the idea of engaging in a scene with some random submissive no longer appealed to him, not with the image of Tori standing in front of him with a flogger in her hand. If he had half a brain at the moment he'd get on his bike and take his sorry ass back home. Unfortunately he understood all too well what would haunt him alone in the dark at this point.

He entered his passcode and then took the stairs two at a time and headed straight to the Masters room. A lot of things might change in a decade but he knew damn well the private enclave reserved for the Purgatory Masters would not. He pulled his keys from his pocket and flipped to the well-worn piece of metal he'd carried with him all these years. As expected, the door opened without a hitch and Levi slipped inside.

There was no need for lights with all the well lit activities filtering up from the first floor being reflected in the one way window that went from floor to ceiling and across the entire back wall of the suite.

Three oversized plush chairs still sat facing the glass and Levi sank down into the first one he reached. The leather had softened with age, making it easy for him to put his head back and stretch his legs in front of him. For days, maybe weeks, he'd been on the go non stop. The more he moved the less he lingered. Now he needed to think. The events of tonight had thrown him for a fucking loop.

She was a Domme.

His mind rebelled at the mere thought. Maybe. He glanced down at the bottle of liquor in his hand and immediately placed it on the floor.

Hell no. He didn't need to drink anymore tonight because he had no intention of camping out here for the night and he'd need all his wits about him to figure out why the hell a woman he barely knew sparked such a visceral reaction in him.

A knock sounded at the door, interrupting his thoughts. As much as he wanted to ignore it, he knew the man on the other side of the door could be persistent.

"Come in."

The door clicked open. "I had a feeling I'd find you in here." Gabe walked in the door and took one of the seats next to him. "I take it the boss or the Dom didn't care for being ordered to my office."

"Fuck no," Levi answered. Neither did he really feel like talking about it at the moment either.

"So if you don't like being given orders do you want to explain why you were about to start a fight to take a turn on the cross? A tiger doesn't change his stripes and neither does a Dom."

"Yeah, hello to you too." Levi didn't want to get into this, but Gabe had known him better than almost anyone and despite the years apart, he wasn't going to let it go.

The other man stretched out his legs and they both stared at the club commotion spread out before them for several minutes. "Place looks good. Different, but good."

"I'll take that as a compliment. I care for her as if she were my own."

"I know you do. If things had turned out differently you wouldn't have to do it on your own."

"Mason handles a lot of the business online. All the financials, the payroll, etc. I enjoy the rest of the job. Including the hiring of each employee."

Gabe's emphasis on employee wasn't lost on him. He'd steered the conversation exactly where he wanted to go. Levi let the silence stretch out for several minutes more before he spoke again. "I met her this morning out at Nina's right after I arrived. I didn't get to spend much time with her but I sure as hell didn't get a Domme vibe from her so accidentally running into her tonight caught me off guard and pissed me the hell off. She doesn't belong here." Levi crossed his arms behind his head and leaned back.

"No disrespect, Levi, but the club isn't anything like it used to be and Mistress Cat is one of the most popular pro Domme's here. When I can get her to take a slot, that is."

Levi lifted his head. "What do you mean? And seriously, Cat? That's the best scene name she could come up with? Although I guess it's better than Tori. A little."

Gabe smiled and shrugged his shoulders. "Her

regular job here is actually next door in the busy restaurant where she works as one of our hostesses five nights a week and maybe you should ask her why we call her Cat."

"I'm happy to hear the restaurant is thriving. Still doesn't mean she belongs here. If she's not submissive I'll eat my boots. A woman like her needs a Dom watching over her. I can feel it."

Gabe laughed so long he practically had tears in his eyes. "Oh this is going to get very interesting. I hope I get to watch."

"Bastard."

"Asshole," he fired back. "Now tell me what's really going on? Cat's a hell of a woman, but I doubt that's why you've returned. Why are you really here?"

Levi pushed to his feet and stood by the window. He'd known coming back out of the blue would raise a lot of questions but that didn't make the process any easier. "I'm probably going to ask myself that same question every time you or Mason or Nina start grilling me." He whirled on Gabe. "I'm only going to say this once and then we're done talking about it." He took a step forward. "I've been to hell on earth multiple times and somehow survived when my sorry ass should have died trying. I've watched my friends die, I've killed some I thought were friends, and still I lived. Now whether I deserve it or not I've come home and I want nothing more than to find an ordinary life. At least as ordinary as someone like me can get. Maybe a family too. Something normal."

Silence stretched between them. The faint sound of the music below ticked the seconds by.

Finally, Gabe held out his arm and opened his hand. Levi remembered the move as he reached for his friend's forearm. Their old fraternity shake. Lost but not forgotten. "I doubt normal will ever suit you, but welcome home, brother."

FIVE

Tori backed away from the door Gabe had left ajar and pushed her back against the wall. Curiosity had driven her to follow behind her boss after he left his office, although she shuddered to think what he'd do to her if she were caught. The rumors of his need to discipline were spread far and wide and employees were often given a choice of the door or the bench. But whatever Levi had started down in the club wasn't going to get dropped, and if they were going to discuss her she wanted to know. Now she'd overheard more than she bargained for and she didn't know how to process it. A chance encounter at Nina's cafe this morning had left her out of sorts and unsettled all day long. Enough that she'd called Gabe and offered to work tonight in the club. A job she had no business taking in this frame of mind. Her only hope had been to work out whatever the hell Levi's sudden presence had done to her and regain her focus.

He'd annoyed her, that's for sure. Even road grime several inches thick and an obvious need of a hot bath with a gallon of soap had not detracted from his good looks. And now that he'd cleaned up he'd turned downright lethal in that department. Her stomach still jolted at the memory of her first good look at Levi in the club. She'd damn near swallowed her tongue. All six foot something of him had exuded a level of innate power she'd felt clear to her bones. It had been so strong she'd glanced around to see if anyone else had noticed.

They had.

Amidst a sea of people in every shape, size and orientation he'd still stood out. Tall and broad shouldered, with dark wavy hair that looked like he'd done nothing more than run his fingers through it with amazing results. He'd trimmed his scruffy beard several inches without removing it altogether and the first thought through her mind had been how would it feel to have that sexy facial hair scratch across her belly or against the inside of her thighs as he...

Damn. When exactly had beards become so sexy?

The moment his piercing blue gaze had met hers across the scarred counter at Nina's, that's when. The appearance of a scruffy stranger sitting with her daughter and coloring together had initially alarmed her. The early warning bells had gone off and her need to protect had taken center stage. Then Hannah had drawn a smile from him that looked both sweet and tortured. The unexpected combination had shaken her to her core.

"Thanks. It's good to be back. I think." She heard Levi's voice just as the door swung open next to her.

Crap. She'd gotten lost in her thoughts and hadn't heard the men approach. Now she was about to get busted for eavesdropping. She swiveled on her ridiculous heels a little too fast and stumbled on the carpet. She reached for the wall and righted herself but not fast enough.

"Stop." The stranger's command came on a low growl far closer than she'd like.

Compelled by his deep voice, she halted in mid-step.

"Come to me," he ordered in a deep dark unholy tone that made her nearly melt on the spot.

"Levi, not a good idea," Gabe warned behind her.

She held her breath. Gabe was the top dog at Purgatory and her boss. Levi would have to defer to him. He'd save her.

"Gabe, I respect your authority here, but in this case I'm going to insist."

Tori sucked in air and waited--and hoped Gabe wasn't about to turn her over to this--this stranger. When the heavy sigh of defeat met her ears she cringed. What the hell?

"Please consider she's one of my best employees. I'd like to keep her." With that Gabe swept past her and descended down the staircase without looking back, leaving her alone with an angry Dom. The word Dom slid sinuously through her system and heated her between her legs.

With her only chance at being saved gone, the silence stretched between them. He'd issued his command and likely wouldn't again. Like most Doms she knew he'd expect for his order to be followed and would wait for the response he sought. She considered her options. Turn around and face the music or flee and probably lose her job.

Her heart beat furiously as she made the only decision she could. Job or no job she was not a coward. She turned and gasped when she discovered him only inches away from her.

When had he moved and how had she not heard him?

"I half expected you to run," he commented.

She lifted her chin. "Then you don't know me very well at all. I don't scare that easily." Although her stomach quivering due to his proximity told a different story. This close to him she noticed the muscles of his shoulders and arms pushing at the seams of his shirt. She easily imagined the hard planes she'd find underneath. And to her surprise the dark tip of another tattoo peeked out from the collar of

ELIZA GAYLE

his shirt. Where exactly did those marks lead? Tori wanted to peel the shirt from him and see the rest. Her obvious weakness for an inked man was pale in comparison to the need surging through her blood as he moved closer.

"Is that right? Then you won't mind this a bit." Before she could react he grabbed her wrist and shackled it with a cuff attached to the wall. While she searched for the right words, he grabbed her opposite hand and followed suit with the second one.

He stood back and surveyed his handiwork with a slight smirk across his face. Tori had an overwhelming urge to smack it off. He had the face of an angel and the attitude of the devil. Arrogant bastard. "Let me go," she demanded.

"I bet you think you have everyone in the club fooled don't you?"

She narrowed her eyes and frowned. "What in the world are you talking about?"

"This." He waved his hand up and down in front of her. "Your get up. It's quite the ruse. Making everyone think you're a Domme. The clothes, your height. It all works in your favor. Until someone decides to take a closer look." He stepped closer and she swore she felt the body heat emanating from him. He stared into her eyes as his fingers blazed a slow trail across her collarbone and into the swell between her breasts. "But you're not a Domme at all, are you?" His warm breath bathed her face. "Only no one takes the time to notice."

With him this close she found it impossible to think straight. What had he asked? Her gaze zeroed in on his lips as he spoke and she wanted nothing more at that moment than to feel them on her skin.

"Tori, or should I call you Cat? Which name is real?"

"Both," she whispered, mesmerized by his lake blue eyes. She didn't think she'd ever met someone with that

52

shade of dark blue before. It would be so easy to get lost...

"What?"

"What?" she repeated, unsure of the question.

"Your name. You said both. Explain yourself now, please."

The added word please felt like an afterthought when he said it, but she liked it anyway.

"My full name is Catori Inola Ford. My friends call me Tori and at work I'm known as Cat. For obvious reasons, I like the separation."

His brow furrowed at the same time he picked up a piece of her hair and wrapped it around his finger. "Catori," he repeated.

She went weak in the knees at his use of her given name. No one outside her family ever called her that, but the way it rolled from his tongue made her want to drop to her knees and beg him to say it again.

"Native American and lovely. That actually makes more sense now. When we met yesterday your name didn't match the woman in front of me. Catori is beautiful. What does it mean? And why don't you use your real name?" He tugged a strand of her hair and brought their faces closer together.

She shrugged, hoping she didn't reveal how much he got to her. "I live in a small community where fitting in means the difference between success and failure. Even in this day and age, not everyone is comfortable with my heritage. So using a nickname simply makes life easier."

He froze, his body going rigid. "That's bullshit. Why would anyone in their right mind be offended by such a thing?"

She shrugged. She wasn't about to get into the hell Hannah's father had put her through when he decided to leave. His angry parting words about her being a dirty mongrel with no morals had been burned into her psyche.

God, he'd fooled them all. Elitist asshole. Nor was she about to tell a stranger the whole truth about why she changed her name. Her business was her business. Period.

"You'd have to ask someone else," she demurred, attempting to turn her head away from him.

"Is that so?" His grip tightened on her hair, effectively imprisoning her. "Well, I'm feeling rather fond of the color of your skin." He brushed the fingers of his free hand along the opposite side of her face. "And the dark eyes staring back at me hold more than a fair share of pent up emotion I'd like to get to the bottom of."

"That sounds nice and all but you're looking for more than is there. I'm not complex or deep. I'm the ultimate what you see is what you get girl. Boring I know, but it's the truth."

He frowned. "Is that what you believe or is that what you tell people to keep them at arm's length? Cause I see a woman who is dressed like a Domme and working as a Domme but doesn't respond at all like a Domme. So tell me, when do I get the truth?"

She bristled at his words. Whether they'd hit home or not didn't really matter. "You have a lot of gall to make so many assumptions about someone you know nothing about."

One of Levi's eyebrows climbed toward his hairline. That look came with a strong warning that said "danger ahead." As much as she hated to admit it, even to herself, his overbearing attitude turned her on. Underneath her tight bustier her nipples had bunched tight and the heat between her legs had spread. How was it he was the first person to finally notice her charade?

"I know you make the most amazing peach pie I've ever tasted and trust me that's saying something. I consider myself a pie connoisseur. And I know you're a great mom. That's something to be especially proud of."

She started to speak and he covered her mouth with his hand to keep her quiet. "Not yet. I haven't finished. I know you're a great mom because after a few minutes with Hannah I realized she is an amazing child. That doesn't come by accident. You're obviously a good friend too, or Nina wouldn't be protecting you like a mother bear. Her stern warning to stay away from you came directly from the friend well. She's the most loyal woman I've ever known and I'd trust her instincts implicitly. And I *know* you're not a Domme."

Tears burned at the back of her eyes as he went down the list of her attributes. It had been far longer than she liked to admit since someone of the male persuasion had noticed. Finally he moved his hand and allowed her to speak. She cleared her throat and prayed she wouldn't betray how much his assessment affected her.

"How can you be so sure?"

"Because I've never wanted a woman more in my life and I can't be wrong. I just can't."

Her mouth dropped open. *Holy Shit.* His honesty stunned her.

She squeezed her eyes shut and started her familiar mantra in her head. He's too good to be true. *He's too good to be true. He's too good to be true.*

Slowly, she opened her eyes and found that vibrant blue gaze fixated on her. Patience. Hope. Need. Strength. She saw it all. Levi was a fucking Dom and he'd set his sights on her.

Tori sagged against the restraints. If she didn't find a way to shut him down now she feared he would pursue her relentlessly. Something she absolutely could not afford getting caught up in again. Anything that meant she lost control would be unacceptable.

"It doesn't matter," she said. "I'm off the market and I intend to stay that way. I do this for my job on occasion and I'm good at it. And the money is good, which is exactly what I need."

"For your pie shop?"

Her mouth dropped open again. What the hell? How did he know so much about her?

A slow smile crawled across his face. "I know more than you thought."

At a loss for words, she wisely kept her mouth shut.

"Do you have a safeword?" he asked.

Her brain went into overdrive at his question. "What? Why?" She breathed deep trying to settle her thoughts in order to form a coherent sentence. "Of course I do. Everyone who works in the VIP areas is required to have a chosen safeword. Mine is Elvis."

The hard planes of Levi's face remained stern, but the twitch at the corner of his mouth gave him away. He was trying to hide a smile.

"You may not be a Domme, but you won't be an easy sub either. Lucky for you I'm up for the challenge. Now tell me, if I reach under this tight miniscule skirt would I find a wet pussy?"

The blood drained from her head at his shocking words. He'd heard her out and simply chosen to ignore everything she'd said. Not to mention the fact he'd zeroed in on her arousal in two seconds flat.

A low chuckle sounded from his delectable throat and the sudden urge to lick and bite him there overwhelmed her. She desperately wanted to discover more of the ink teasing the edges of his neck. Maybe Nina was right. She needed to get laid.

He leaned closer, pressing his mouth against the shell of her ear. "Would you drench my hand if I ordered you to your knees to suck my dick as penance for your eavesdropping? Or would you beg for my fingers to get you off first? Watching a sweet submissive beg for what she wants is one of my favorite things to see."

Tori gasped. Shock seized her insides as Levi's voice flowed through her. Shit. Shit. Shit. Now she couldn't get the idea of his hard length pushing into her mouth out of her mind. She imagined his hands wrapped in her thick hair controlling how deep or shallow she took him in. As he'd guessed, moisture drenched her thong. Damn him.

It had been so long since she'd truly been with a man. Actually, until this morning it had been easy to ignore her dormant needs. She'd easily put aside a personal life for the sake of her daughter and as normal a life as she could give her. They'd started out their life here flat broke with only a small roof over their head. Over the years, she'd worked hard to save money and make sure her child needed for nothing. And when she was lucky, she made enough extra to put away for the future.

"Focus, Catori. Don't let your mind wander to anything but what's happening right now." He surged forward and the hard length of his erection pushed against her stomach.

Her eyes rolled toward the back of her head. So big. And hot. She wanted to succumb. It would be so easy… Like riding a bike.

"Stand still and spread your legs."

To her shock she obeyed. Something about him made her lose her mind. "This isn't right," she whispered. Yet somehow the need to deny him only fed the excitement still building inside her.

"Whether it's right or not is no longer up to you, my little Catori. Your body has already betrayed you and given me a glimpse of your need." He reached between her legs and touched her inner thigh. "How can I, as a good Dom, neglect that?"

The sound of her gasp filled the hallway, reminding her just how public this could be. Anyone with membership status could come up the stairs and find her like this. Another thought that should have scared the piss out of her but only fueled the excitement.

His fingers burned a path straight to the edge of her thong. He pushed aside the fabric and slid between the lips of her sex. With the touch of an expert he explored her aching flesh as if he'd known her forever. She rolled her hips, urging him to take more.

"If I take my hand away now, will you beg for more?"

"Of course not," she lied.

This time his deep chuckle vibrated across her skin and sent a zing to her nipples. He made her ache for things she had no business asking for. This wasn't her. At least not anymore.

He shifted his hand and she held her breath in fear that he'd stop. Instead he shoved her thong out of his way and pushed a finger deep inside her.

Tori cried out. Her loss of control had take a giant leap off the side of the smart cliff and if she didn't do something quick there would be no return. Sex she could handle, maybe even embrace. Him getting inside her head? That thought sobered her despite the crazed sensations his finger created inside her. She had a safeword that guaranteed escape or she could work a different approach.

She fought for a sense of control long enough to gather a few last words that might stop the avalanche. "This is where I should be a good little submissive, right?"

As she'd predicted his hand stilled and his eyes narrowed. The need to give into him threatened to overtake her. She did want to be the good little submissive. On her knees. Cock in her mouth.

With the best smirk she could muster she stared into his eyes, "May I please suck you," she hesitated long enough to let the sarcasm sink in. "Sir."

SIX

Levi pulled back and stared into her dark brown eyes with the gold flecks that made his stomach quiver. When had he let things get out of control? He'd only planned to prove his point that she was not a Dominant. A wet pussy in his hand and a woman willing to suck his dick had not been part of the plan. And she was willing all right. Despite the sarcasm her face flushed with arousal and her legs trembled against his hand. Fuck.

"As much as I would love to accept your gracious offer, I'm afraid you're not ready. You've decided to have sex with me tonight because your body craves it and you figure why not scratch the itch and be done with it, right?"

She simply shrugged and Levi knew he'd hit the bulls eye.

"When you and I fuck, and make no mistake we will, it won't just be some random sex. You'll have chosen me as someone you honestly want to submit to with both your body and your mind."

Her eyes flashed with a myriad of emotions from hurt to anger in a matter of seconds. "If you're so sure about me then let me go."

"Not even a please?" he asked. Her lips clamped shut and she stared at him with volumes of defiance. Her spirit fired his blood and totally turned him on. "Well, unfortunately for you, you're in no position to make demands." He withdrew his fingers and brought his hand to his mouth. "I should make you suck my fingers clean, but why deny myself the taste I'm dying for?"

Her whimpered response satisfied him more than any words could. But he wasn't prepared for the full out whine from her when he licked his fingers clean one at a time. Damn. She tasted as tart and perfect as her attitude. Sure, she needed some training but the basic responses came naturally and that's what really mattered. With a loud pop he pulled his second finger free and fought the urge to yank her skirt over her hips and bury himself inside her. That's all his brain could focus on. Being balls deep inside this contrary, beautiful, responsive, submissive woman.

He took the three steps that separated them and went after her, devouring her mouth. Her head fell back under the pressure and he inhaled every square inch of her he could. With a sexy mewl she acquiesced to his unspoken demand and opened for more access. He shoved deep and explored the recesses of her hot mouth with the same single-minded intensity as if they were fucking. The need to get so deep inside her nothing from the outside would matter continued to ride him hard. But if she was going to walk away from him tonight then he'd be damn sure she fully understood what that meant. The sound of her hands jerking on the restraints pulsed in his cock. Nothing like a woman who got lost in the moment enough to struggle and plead for more of what he wanted to give her. If she were free now, he'd likely feel the rake of her nails along his back or the easy slide of her hand across the bulge in his pants.

He ripped his mouth from hers and buried his face in her neck. The sweet scent of honey and sugar on her skin permeated his brain and threatened his ability to keep from pounding into her where they stood. If he touched anything more at the moment he'd be done for. What would it do to him when he finally slid his cock inside her?

"Levi," the soft plead and arch of her hips were filled with so much desire and need he had to grit his teeth against the ache to devour her from head to toe. Her easy response under his command made her all the more desirable. Walking away now would drive him insane.

"Fuck," he swore and pulled away, giving them both some much needed space. "You don't understand my little, Catori. If we go forward from here, I'm going to want full access to you. And beyond that, I'll make demands on your mind and body that will push you to every physical and emotional limit. I'm not an easy lover. Are you ready for that?"

It had been so long since he'd wanted anything more than a night or two from a woman. A year ago the thought would have sent him running, tonight he could only picture Catori at his feet with sass in her gaze and desire in her heart.

She stared at him for a long time, the indecision clear on her face. It took every bit of restraint he possessed not to override her hesitation with a simple command. It wouldn't take much to have her mindless and underneath him.

"That's what I thought." He stepped back, disappointment coursing through him.

"You don't understand. We can't do this. Not because I don't want it, though. My life can't be this anymore... Just forget it." Her head dropped forward and her shoulders sagged. The aura of defeat emanating from her robbed him of common sense. She needed him far more than she knew.

"Look at me, Catori." He loved the sound of her name when he spoke it. It was as exotic as the woman he craved.

She didn't move so long he feared she'd chosen to disobey him. Finally her head lifted and she met his gaze. Some of her earlier starch had returned.

"Why can't we? You don't want a demanding Dom? That's what it'll take to have what you need."

"Demanding in the bedroom I can handle, trust me, but we barely know each other and I simply can't handle complicated. It's taken me a long time to get where I am and change now could destroy everything."

He touched her cheek and wiped at the small tear that escaped one eye. "I can only imagine how hard it is to be a single working mother. But you're doing a fantastic job. You're right that I don't know you well, but I want to." He cupped her cheek. "I've seen a lot of bad stuff in this world. Too much, actually. But one thing I've learned is that at some point you have to take care of yourself or those around you will suffer for it."

"Easier said than done," she blurted.

He moved his fingers beneath her chin and lifted her head until her neck stretched high. "When was the last time you've done this?"

Immediately her face and neck flushed. He didn't need her answer to know it had been far too long.

"That doesn't matter," she insisted.

"Maybe it does, maybe it doesn't but you've got to know the most important part of a relationship between a Dominant and submissive is open communication." He stepped closer and lowered his voice. "How long?"

She tried to turn her head so she didn't have to meet his gaze and he tightened his grip. He wasn't about to let her go without an answer. "No, you can't be afraid to tell me or embarrassed or anything else. I'm not planning to judge you, I simply need to know you."

His mind raced with the possibilities for why this beautiful woman had closed herself to a sexual relationship with a dominant man. Although the idea of reintroducing her to the pleasure of submission at his hand tightened his cock to the point of sweet pain. He breathed deeply, enjoying the hell out of the familiar sensation. His chest constricted, his heart raced. Finally.

With a telltale dark flush of embarrassment on her skin and a dip of her head to hide her eyes, she finally replied, "I haven't had sex in almost two years."

Shock slammed his chest. His blood flashed hot and headed south. His fingers flexed with the need to wrap his hand around her throat and hold her tight while he pushed inside her. Air clogged in his lungs and his brain misfired at the image of reintroducing her to the darker pleasures of sex.

He pulled himself together. "Close, but not exactly what I meant. How long since you've engaged in D/s?"

She visibly swallowed, the fear building in her eyes. He wanted to shake her with the truth that nothing she said would be condemned. Nothing.

"Almost eight years ago. Before I met Hannah's father. Are you happy now? Now can I go?"

Levi stared at her, really looked while his brain calculated the math. Hannah had mentioned she'd just turned five and Tori didn't look a day over twenty-five. But that would mean she'd only been...

"How old are you?" He had to know. Wondering would drive him mad if he didn't know it all.

Her spine straightened and she lifted her head. Damn he loved the fierce pride that filled her when faced with something questionable.

"Anyone ever told you how impolite that question is?"

"No," probably because he'd never needed to ask.

She shook her head. "Fine. I can tell by the look on your face you'll figure it out whether I tell you or not. But first uncuff me."

His mouth had gone dry. Whatever it was he'd forced out of her had stuck in his stomach like a lead weight. Catori Inola Ford was no ordinary submissive. He reached for her wrist and granted her request. He took several long minutes to massage and kiss each of her wrists before finally releasing her. She looked at him with those emotional dark eyes and he ached to get inside her and learn what made her tick.

Despite the clear standoff vibe, he pulled her into his arms. He had to touch her. Not long after, her muscles began to loosen and she rested her cheek on his shoulder and wrapped her arms around his waist. It was on the tip of his tongue to grill her for more information when he realized he wanted this moment more. The quiet silence of her in his arms seeking a modicum of comfort. This wasn't right. He'd seen the grief and fear in her eyes. Whatever she'd been about to tell him deserved more than a rough exploration in the hallway of Purgatory.

"Come to dinner with me," he blurted. "We'll talk there."

"I can't," she whispered against his shirt. "It's after midnight. The babysitter is expecting me right about now."

The weight of her responsibilities brought them both back to reality. He pulled back and held her at arm's length. He didn't want to talk to her back. He enjoyed watching her reactions far too much. "Tomorrow then. We'll go out."

She shook her head. "I can't." She was beginning to sound like a broken record. "I have pies to bake, a child to watch and I work at the restaurant tomorrow night."

He started to tell her that he'd get her the night off and stopped. She wasn't ready for that information yet. "Restaurant closes at what? Ten?"

"Midnight."

Dammit. He wanted to take her home now. Lay her down on her bed, hold her hands above her head and fuck her so deep she'd beg for everything he'd give. He willed his cock to stop putting ideas like that in his head. He needed to take this slow for now. "Fine, I'll pick you up at midnight and take you home. Do you need a ride home tonight?"

"No, I drove."

Reluctant for the night to end, he grabbed her hand and placed a kiss on her palm. "Dream of me tonight, Catori. You've managed your reprieve but rest assured it is only temporary." He opened his mouth and grazed his teeth sharply against the thin skin of her wrist. She rewarded him with a whimper and he finally released her.

She turned and started down the hall toward the stairs and he let his gaze fall to her full rear end. His cock leapt in her direction, clear on what it wanted. "Down boy. Not yet."

Tori turned back, catching him off guard. Had she heard him?

"Are you in the mood for pie?" she asked.

He perked up immediately. "Sweetheart, I am always in the mood for pie. Are you offering?"

"I baked some fresh earlier today. It's not dinner but I can probably scrounge up some sandwich fixings."

"Sold." He caught up with her in three strides. "Lead the way, darlin."

"I could get used to that," she purred. "Leading the way I mean."

He laughed before his voice went low. "Don't get too used to it," he brushed his thumb across her delectable mouth. "When this is all over, I will be in control."

SEVEN

Tori tried not to watch Levi devour his second piece of pie, but every time he lifted the fork to his mouth and opened those gorgeous lips of his she wanted to climb up in his lap and get that same attention on her. The thought of him running that tongue along her neck or grazing his teeth… Oh fuck that. She wanted him to bite her. When was the last time someone wanted her bad enough to go that far?

He'd followed her home from Purgatory and now she couldn't stop thinking about him following her to the bedroom. All this sex on the brain was slowly killing her.

Finally Levi pushed his plate away and rubbed his stomach. "Damn, that was good."

She knew he meant her food, but her mind had left the table long ago. Levi sparked an entirely different kind of hunger inside her.

"What are you thinking?" He came around the table and pulled her into his arms. "Tell me."

"Nothing. Just happy you like the pie."

"Don't lie, Catori." His voice deepened and her body went on high alert. The way he said her full name instantly changed the mood in the room. Play time was over.

Or maybe it was just getting started. A girl could hope.

"I am really glad you like my baking." The short sentence came out heavy as she fought for air. His right hand had started to caress the small of her back and it wasn't easy to keep her thoughts straight.

"I'm sure you do, but that is not what you were thinking. Now be honest or we'll have to do this the hard way."

She blinked at him. Did she want to know what the hard way was? A shiver worked along her spine. Not yet. "I was thinking about your teeth."

A small smile quirked the edges of his mouth making him look even sexier if that were possible. "My teeth? Seriously?"

"Yes, seriously." She tried to push against his chest and found a wall of immovable muscle. "For a split second of obvious insanity I wondered what it would feel like if you bit me with them." She tried to pull away again and he tightened her flat against him. When the hot, hard length of his erection aligned and pushed against her mound, her gaze flew to his and the dark depths of his arousal flooded her.

"You like pain." It wasn't a question. Simply a statement uttered in a husky, desire-roughened voice. A sound that zipped through her and straight to parts she was supposed to be ignoring.

"No. That's not what I meant." She struggled and after a few impossible seconds he released her. Tori stumbled a few steps back, grabbing onto the island for support.

"I know exactly what you meant but I think we should talk before we finish that conversation. You never did answer my question earlier."

Shit. She really didn't want to go through this. "What question?"

His left brow lifted. "Don't be that woman, Catori. I

won't play games with you and I won't tolerate games from you either. Let's do this like the adults we are. Otherwise I might as well go home now."

Her shoulders sagged a fraction. He was right of course, not that it made her feel any better to admit it. She could either tell him what he wanted to know or say goodnight and let it go. Before her brain had settled on an answer she leaned on the counter and opened her mouth. "I turned twenty-six last month." She could wait and let him do that math or just get it over with and tell him.

"Yes, I was eighteen when my last D/s relationship ended." To her ears the words landed in the room with the subtlety of a grenade. To his credit, his facial features remained still and very little reaction showed on his face. However, for her the memories came racing back and the threat of tears made her look away from him.

"Catori."

He spoke her name, this time not in desire but with a strong dose of sympathy inside it.

"No, please don't do that. You should probably let me finish before you start feeling sorry for me. It's not at all what you might think." She took a deep breath and continued before he interrupted. "My parents divorced when I was ten after my dad fell in love with a new woman. My mother was so heartbroken we left the reservation and moved here. Far enough away so she wouldn't have to see them on a regular basis but still close enough that I could spend weekends and summers with my grandparents."

She took a deep breath and steeled her heart before she continued. "When I was fourteen she met a new man and decided to get married again. My stepfather was a kind man. A good man that any woman would be lucky to have. He took us both in and treated me as if I were his own daughter. Much better than I could have hoped. He had a son from his first marriage that was in the army at the time.

In fact he was deployed when they got married so I didn't
even meet him for quite some time. Unfortunately, my mom
never really got over my father and she started drinking.
Heavily. When I turned sixteen she left and went into rehab.
The first of many times she went to rehab. My stepfather
did the best he could to take care of me, but I got pretty
wild as a teenager. On my seventeenth birthday I met a man
several years older than me and fell head over heels for him.
He introduced me to BDSM and for a year and a half I was
convinced I'd found where I belonged. Then it ended. I
decided to put all that behind me and not long after I met
Hannah's father. The rest is pretty typical. Got pregnant, got
married, got divorced. Now here I am doing my own thing
and doing it pretty well I think."

For a second Levi looked a bit shell shocked and
distant. She wondered if he'd even heard everything she
said. She started to get up and his hand snaked out and
grabbed hers. "How did it end?"

Old grief cut through her psyche. Those were doors
she couldn't open again. "It just did. Okay. Life happens.
People move on."

The look on his face clearly said he didn't believe
her and she forced herself to shrug it off. She'd known this
man less than twenty-four hours and she'd bared half her
soul to him. She wasn't about to give him the other half. A
quick glance at the clock on the wall reminded her that
Hannah would be up and raring to go in less than five
hours. "Look, I think we should call it a night. Hannah is an
early riser and I'm going to need some rest before another
long day starts." She walked toward the door and prayed
he'd follow.

He did. "What do you want now?"

"I don't know. Until this morning I was perfectly
fine with my life as it is and then meeting you turned
everything upside down."

"Good. Stand still." When she obeyed his command he smiled. "I can give you what you need, but you have to choose to submit to me. You have to say the words. When you do, we'll take the time to get to know each other ... my way."

She swallowed against the lump that formed in her throat. "Your way?"

He nodded. "Yes. My rules, my decisions, my control."

Despite the many years that had passed since she'd dared to give up control, her body reacted instinctively. Her nipples bunched and scraped against her bra and the pressure between her legs magnified ten fold. The man standing in front of her with his dark blue eyes full of intent and tattoos that probably covered his body knew exactly what he was doing to her. He knew.

She rolled that thought around in her head as her body swayed. He grabbed her bottom and pulled their bodies together once again. "There are a hundred different things I could do to your body that would make you scream and beg, but every one will be with your consent." He lifted her leg and positioned her so that the ridge of his erection connected with her sex. "Don't get me wrong. This won't be you topping from the bottom, ever. Consent I require, but after that I won't ask for permission again. I'll take what I want and give what you need. Your body and your pleasure will be mine and mine alone." He nudged forward making direct contact with her clit through nothing more than the thin shorts she'd changed into.

"Do you understand?"

"Yes," the word came out broken. She cleared her throat and tried again. "Yes, I think I do."

"Good." He released her leg and took a step back, keeping his hand on her arm so she didn't lose her balance. "Take a couple of days to consider what you want. When you decide, let me know."

He slipped from her house and left her standing there in total, utter shock. The confidence that exuded from him left behind an aura she could almost bathe in. *Damn.* He made her want things she knew were not meant for her. Sex was one thing. She'd been ready to end that drought tonight when he'd restrained her at the club. If only he'd gone for the easy one night stand she'd gotten stuck in her head.

Tori looked around her neat as a pin kitchen and tried to think about what she wanted. She already had a beautiful little girl, a budding career as a pie maker and a few carefully chosen friends that kept her from going insane when her life overwhelmed her.

What do you want?

She heard his question over and over in her head as she turned off the lights one by one and went down the hall to her bedroom. She peeked into Hannah's room and watched her chest rise and fall a few times. Satisfied her child was safe and sleeping, she entered her room and removed the clothes that had been making her crazy since Levi touched her. She knew from experience that even her nightgown would irritate her sensitized skin. As she sank into her mattress she caught a glimpse of her naked and flushed body in the dresser mirror. She stared at the image and tried to understand what she saw.

What do you want?

The question haunted her as she realized she'd not seen the woman in the mirror since she'd lost her first love, Seth.

Shit. What did she want?

EIGHT

Tucker Lewis stared through the darkness to the window illuminated by the full moon casting its shadow far and wide. The apartment he shared with his submissive Maggie had an incredible view of college campus gardens and at the moment he saw none of it. He'd eagerly followed Maggie north to Boston for the temporary teaching position she'd been offered at a local college. Now the news Nina had dumped on him from home complicated everything.

She'd called to let him know that the long lost Levi had turned up at the lake. His intentions were unclear other than he'd made it crystal he wanted his old life back. He'd even moved back into his childhood home and started renovations. Actually, his normally calm sister had seemed particularly out of sorts over the latest turn of events, which worried him more than anything. If Mason couldn't keep Levi under control he might have to return to North Carolina to run interference. Just like old times. Back in college the three of them had been virtual strangers until they'd had to work together on the football team. After that they'd been inseparable.

For a few years, they were all normal living day to day just like everyone else. Tucker's sardonic laugh at that bullshit boomed through the empty space. Three egotistical men barely old enough to drink banding together to create a secret fraternity that later morphed into the region's largest public and exclusive kink club hardly qualified as normal. Each one of them had been born to be fucked up.

Maggie was due home any minute and he didn't yet have a plan for handling this mess. He'd left out a shitload of details from his past and his day of reckoning had finally arrived. Tucker sighed. The whole fucking situation had turned into one dramatic mess after another and he hated drama almost as much as he hated lying to Maggie.

One of the main reasons he enjoyed so many hours every day in his studio was for the sole purpose of the quiet peace his mind found there. He didn't waste his time on the what if's there. Instead he embraced every hot sweaty minute with the glass. It gave him immense satisfaction to control and manipulate his art. He lived his life that way as well. It was only when other people got involved things got messy. He shook his head in an attempt to knock loose his maudlin thoughts. He'd already wasted too many years in the pit of self pity and he had no desire to go back there.

These past months with Maggie had been the best of his life and selfish or not he had no intention of letting her walk away. He'd fight for her with everything he had in his arsenal before that happened. Of course he could already hear the "I told you so" from Mason running through his head in hi def audio. The man had been his best friend--hell, only friend for more years than he cared to count. His loyalty appeared limitless and Tucker owed his sanity to the other man. Which didn't change the fact that Mason was still a bastard of the first order on a good day.

It kind of came with the job. As Mason had reminded him on more than one occasion, they lived in a state of controlled chaos and he held the reins. Unfortunately, their tightly held secrets had a few loose ends dangling, namely Tucker and Levi, and all it would take was one hard tug to send them all spiraling.

He simply had to come clean with Maggie tonight. At least on what he could. He'd stand tall and admit there were some dirty secrets still hiding in his deep closet that may affect them both very soon. Thank God the reporters had finally quit tracking their every move. The reclusive billionaire son of one of the country's notorious televangelists living with the female college professor who'd been arrested in a BDSM club raid had attracted far more attention than he and Maggie had anticipated. The many calls from Mason reaming his ass over each and every news story splashed across the tabloids had gotten old quick. They'd both agreed he'd stay away from North Carolina, his sister, and the Purgatory club until it completely died down. Eventually it had. When a much younger blue-blooded playboy had been implicated in a huge hotel sex scandal in Las Vegas, the reporters darkening his door step had packed up and headed for the shark infested waters of fresh meat.

Not that the pending storm of Miss Maggie boded well for his future either. He might end up wishing those reporters would return once she got done with him. He'd need the company. She might be submissive to him in the bedroom, but the minute she got wind of the half-truths he'd spoon fed her...

Shit.

The sound of the penthouse elevator swooshing open echoed through the entrance hall of the apartment, followed by the click of Maggie's heels against the marble floor. Tucker immediately pictured her as she'd left their home this morning. She'd emerged from the bathroom wearing yet another one of those prim and proper business suits she liked to wear to class that never failed to get him hot and bothered. His dick perked up. Those tight slim skirts hugged her curvy ass to perfection, but it was the silky thigh highs and garter belts she always wore underneath that undid him. Little did her students know that their buttoned up teacher wore lingerie under those fucking suits that would scorch a man's eyeballs. He shifted in his seat as the head of his cock pressed painfully against the zipper of his pants.

Tonight he'd sit Maggie down and tell her more about him than he'd told anyone ever before, but first he'd take from her what he simply couldn't get enough of. Her touch. The way her fingers spread across his shoulders when he loomed above her, or the way her sharp little nails dug into his back on that first deep thrust. His blood surged through his veins at the thought. Fuck yes.

"Tucker?" she called out to him, her voice a tad on the hesitant side. She'd probably spotted him and sensed something was up with him. He didn't usually sit in the dark and stare out the windows.

"Come," he ordered. A moment of silence followed his command in which he held his breath and waited.

"Yes, Sir," she answered.

He listened to her drop her purse and briefcase on the hall desk and proceed to where he sat. She rounded the chair and a sense of relief swept over him. Not a day went by he didn't appreciate the fact that his Maggie had returned to him. His gaze drifted to her fuck me shoes and a half smile formed across his face. The one indulgence from him she never turned down were those damned sexy shoes. These were black patent and at least four inches high. And even the little strap that buckled around her ankle was hot as hell. From there he followed the line of her stockings where they slipped under the edge of her slim gray skirt. Tucker fought the urge to adjust himself.

When he finally met her eyes with his, he hesitated for several long seconds, drawing out the anticipation. Their relationship had progressed organically over the weeks they'd spent living together, exploring the D/s connection they shared and he was damn proud of them both. Until every time he remembered how little she really knew about him. God, he was so sick of secrets.

"What's wrong?" Her simple question pulled him from his inner turmoil and put his attention back on her where it belonged. They'd get into the details soon enough, but right now they both needed this.

"On your knees, baby. I need you."

Heat flared in her eyes as she moved to comply. She'd already divulged to him how crazy it made her when he got like this. She peeled her jacket from her shoulders and tossed it to the chair opposite him. "Do you want the rest of my clothes off now, Sir?" she asked.

"Just the skirt and top. Leave everything else including the garter and shoes." He couldn't hide the sudden husky tone of his voice. Nor did he want to. Half the fun was getting Maggie so worked up she'd beg, borrow and plead for his cock. He savored every delectable moment of the anticipation.

She must have sensed what he had in mind as she took her sweet time with each tiny button holding her thin silk shirt together. His hands flexed and tightened on the arms of the chair as he half considered ripping the clothes from her body. The war between impatience and the need to savor raged inside him and he wasn't sure which one would win out in the end.

Finally she parted her shirt and he got his first glimpse of the creamy swells of her breasts showcased by the baby blue lace of her peek-a-boo bra. A strangled half groan sounded in his throat. A wanton smile crossed her face as he realized she knew exactly what she did to him with her endless choices in racy undergarments.

The clever minx took a step back and cupped her tits. The deep crease of her cleavage made him want to push his cock between them, maybe come all over her tight, rosy nipples. All too soon, she dropped her breasts and smoothed her hands from ribs to thighs, drawing his attention to the barely-there scrap of panties covering her pussy that would welcome him inside the silken heat.

"I think I said knees, Miss Maggie." His brain was melting fast. Soon, he wouldn't remember what the hell he'd said. Tucker took control by grabbing her wrists and clasping them together in front of her. He didn't have to tug much to begin her descent to the floor. A slight shiver worked over her as her knees hit the floor and he knew he had Maggie right where she wanted to be.

He let go of one hand and guided the other to his pants. "Suck me, baby."

Her eyes widened with a flare of pleasure as she immediately unfastened his pants and lowered the zipper. She wrapped her fingers around his cock and pulled him free. He hissed as brutal need tore through him. "Hurry, Maggie," he insisted.

With a smile on her face she leaned forward and licked him from root to just under the tip before she pulled him free from his pants. That single swipe sent a jolt of electricity racing up his spine. Again he had to grab the arms of the chair to stop himself from throwing her to the ground and shoving into her from behind.

Before his thoughts caught up with her actions she engulfed his penis until it nudged the back of her throat. The automatic tightening of her throat on the head of his cock nearly blew his head off. Jesus H this woman was simply magnificent. He curved his palm around the back of her head and pressed her a fraction deeper before allowing her to pull back. The slow drag of her flattened tongue along the underside of his erection felt every bit as sinful as the back of her throat. She deserved a reward.

He leaned forward and pinched her nipple between

two fingers and tugged it taut. The resulting moan vibrated across his cock and straight into his balls. Between the wet heat and the buzz of sound across his aching flesh he wondered how long he'd be able to hold back from her. Her movements continued in a synchronized execution of sucking and laving that had him bucking his hips and slamming deeper into her mouth. Holy hell, she was a goddess. So much pleasure. He threaded his fingers through her short dark locks and gripped tight. This gave him the leverage he needed to thrust harder against her throat.

"Yes, Maggie. Deeper." Her gaze met his as she stretched her lips to give him better access. The love and trust staring up at him unraveled him farther. As if that wasn't enough, she hollowed her cheeks and sucked harder at his shaft. The pressure raised the stakes as he fought to get deeper inside her. She was really getting into the process now. Her head bobbed up and down as she increased the tempo of her attention all while her tongue worked overtime circling the head and the nerve-rich underside.

"Damn, woman. Don't stop." Shit. She was about to obliterate his control and make him come down her throat. As incredible as that sounded, he wasn't ready to end this yet. They'd barely begun and he wanted to reclaim his submissive in more ways than one before they dredged up the past. He savored the hot slide of her mouth for a few last seconds, clinging to the incredible sensations. Gritting his teeth, he fisted her hair tight and pulled her off his dick.

Her protesting whimper sliced through his restraint. Tucker slanted his mouth over hers and swallowed her cries. Every sound, every whimper she made tonight belonged to him. *Him.* And he intended to savor them.

"On your feet, baby." He watched her scramble and totter for a moment on the heels before she got her bearings and stood. She stared down at him with glassy eyes and swollen red lips. Looking at her was like looking at every wet dream he'd ever had all rolled into one. "You're fucking beautiful, Maggie." He unfolded from the chair and did his best to hide the fact that she'd made his legs turn to rubber. His heart hurt with the love he had for her and the thought of her turning away from him for any reason made him a little crazy.

"Tucker," she started but he couldn't take that part of tonight's program yet. He covered her mouth with his hand and leaned down to her ear. The spicy scent of arousal surrounded him. "No more words, little one. Not unless I ask you a direct question. Understood?"

"Yes, Sir."

"Good." He fingered the clasp between her breasts and slid the latch free. Her tits spilled into his hands and Tucker turned his gaze to the beautiful sight. There wasn't an inch of her body he didn't worship, no matter how much she liked to protest about her imagined too big this or too small that. He couldn't have dreamt a more perfect woman.

One at a time he sucked a nipple into his mouth and swirled his tongue around the puckered skin. Her body swayed and he wrapped an arm around her waist to steady her. He sucked on the tender skin of each sinful orb until her head lolled back and her pants came hard and heavy. With the long column of her throat stretched and exposed, his attention was drawn to the collar she wore around her neck. Like the night he'd given it to her, he felt the surge of possession threatening to overcome him. "You're mine, Maggie. Mind, body and soul. You belong to me now. Whatever happens, no matter how many fucking reporters pursue us, this is mine. Never doubt that." He slipped his fingers underneath the chain and tugged. A moan slipped from her throat and went straight to his cock. He sucked a nipple into his mouth and bit down. The flash of pain made her cry out and he repeated it on the other.

The need to get inside her was clawing at him.

"Stand up, baby." He waited for her to gather her strength before releasing her. "I want you to wrap yourself around the arm of my chair, ass high and head down on the cushion. And spread your legs as wide as you can."

Tucker watched her comply as he tore at his trousers and shoved them down his legs. His shirt quickly followed until he stood naked and proud at the sight before him. Damn. How fucking lucky could one man be? Maybe if he got so deep inside her she'd never leave him no matter what she learned.

A small growl formed in his throat. "Don't move." He hurried to the bedroom and grabbed a few needed supplies before returning to her side. Her eyes widened at the items in his hands but she remained still and didn't utter a sound.

He placed everything on the table except for the tie. "Hands behind your back, my love." Standing behind her, he wrapped the silk tie around her wrists several times before fastening it with a quick slip knot. "Too tight?" he asked.

"No, Master. It's perfect." The change in tone and the use of Master indicated his Miss Maggie was slipping deep into submissive mode.

He leaned forward and whispered at her ear. "I'm going to fuck you so hard. So thoroughly that the sensation of my cock deep inside you will forever be imprinted in your mind. When you wake up every day it will be the first thing in your head. My cock, Maggie. You'll crave it every fucking day."

"I already do," she cried.

He reared back. "Was that a question? Did I give you permission to speak?" Before she had a chance to answer, he landed a powerful swat across the middle of her ass. And another and another. Her gorgeous white ass bloomed red and he imagined the burn making its way across her skin. The sight only fueled the need already tearing him in two. He grabbed the straps of her thong and roughly pulled it halfway down her legs. Her bare pussy was already wet and swollen with her arousal. *Shit.* The heady scent hit him square in the chest like a ton of bricks, making him nearly fall to his knees. His already painful erection throbbed mercilessly.

Confident she'd received the message about talking, he drove two fingers deep into her seeping pussy. The tight clasp of her muscles melted his brain. Not to mention the heat now scalding his hand. His heart beat furiously as he tried to maintain a modicum of control. He almost laughed out loud. Touching Maggie never made it easy to stay composed. He worked his fingers around the silken walls of her channel until she gasped. Oh yeah. There is was. He stroked that spot over and over, taunting her with the extreme pleasure.

"Do you want to be fucked or do you think we should stop?"

"Oh God no. Please, Master. I want to be fucked."

"Mmm. I'll definitely take that into consideration." He pulled his fingers from her clasp and used both hands to spread her ass cheeks. Her rosette clinched. She knew what was coming. Tucker bent and rimmed the tiny hole with his tongue. She gasped and clenched again. He smiled and worked his mouth to the fleshy part of her backside. Not matter what she said or did, they both knew how much she loved when he did this to her.

"Should I stop?"

"Fuck no," she wailed.

Tucker took his time and laved the sensitive flesh repeatedly. He added one finger to the process and worked her open. Her fists clenched so tight her knuckles turned white. He'd shown her many times these past weeks just how sensitive these nerve endings were and she'd often begged for more.

Ready to take this another step forward, he yanked the tube of lube he'd brought in with his supplies. He squeezed some on his fingers and then massaged it all over her rosette. He hadn't planned to fuck her there tonight but after he claimed her pussy, he might need a second round. One last plunge of two fingers inside her ass left Maggie gasping and squirming on the edge of the chair.

He reached for the large red plug she'd spied in his hands and slathered it with the slick gel. This little beauty was a size larger than she was used to and perfect for what he wanted for her tonight. He lined the tip of the toy with her little puckered ring and pressed gently forward. As he'd trained her, she didn't tense up or freeze. She pressed out and he slid one inch at a time into her ass as he stroked her rigid clit. At the widest point of the flared plug her muscles began to shake.

"Relax, my love. Imagine what it's going to feel like with my cock in your cunt and this plug in your ass."

"Ohhh," she cried out and he buried the toy to the hilt. Without breaking their connection, Tucker stood back and admired her splayed out before him. Hands tied behind her back, legs spread wide, toy up her ass and her pussy dripping in anticipation. He thanked his lucky stars and prayed the woman he didn't deserve never left him.

He stepped forward and pressed his erection against the inside of her thigh. Her heat radiated through him and Tucker knew she'd kill him tonight. "You look and feel amazing. I can't wait another second to be inside you."

He positioned himself behind her and nudged her sodden folds. She whimpered, the sound rolling up and down his spine in pure delight. His hands grabbed her hips and began to push inside her. She squirmed and tensed. "Ohh. Ohh," she murmured

"I know, baby. It's fucking tight." The desperation

to be inside her now clawed at his mind and he fought for restraint. He needed to take this nice and slow so as not to hurt her but not an easy task when he could barely see straight. "Just relax," he urged, just shy of begging himself.

He worked in a bit deeper and dark spots flashed in front of his eyes. The toy in her ass made her pussy impossibly tight. He was halfway in and already the ecstasy of the snug fit blew his mind. He breathed through the urge to force his way in. He leaned forward and draped over her back so he could reach around and pluck at a nipple. She had many erogenous zones, especially these. When she'd originally told him her nipples weren't that sensitive, he'd quickly proven her wrong with a pair of evil little nipple clamps.

As if reading his mind, her breath came out in short, hard pants and a rush of arousal covered his shaft. With the added lubrication he eased forward another inch.

"Oh--Master--more."

"We're almost there. Take some deep breaths and relax. I'm trying to be gentle but dammit, I need to use you."

Those final five words did it. Her brain focused on that and her body stopped fighting his entrance. He slid all the way to the hilt and his brain exploded at the sinful pleasure flowing over him. A growl tore from his throat as his hands gripped her hips hard to keep him from moving too fast.

"Tell me, baby. Tell me how it feels."

"Oooohhhh," she wailed. "So full. Oh my God. Never been like this."

Her hard fought words were music to his ears. He eased back, then plowed deep inside her again, her gasp nearly all the reward he needed. He couldn't stop now, she felt too incredible. He stroked in and out of her, the hard press of the plug applying amazing pressure against his shaft.

Any doubt he'd lose his mind, disappeared. Every time she tightened on him it pulled him one step closer to coming. His body already burned with the desire, but not until he got her there with him. "Keep talking to me, Maggie. Tell me what you want."

"Harder," she cried.

That single word ignited his cock. He withdrew and shoved inside her again so hard the chair groaned instead of Maggie. The intensity of sensation made his eyes roll to the back of his head.

"Please. Help. Oh God. Too good." Her constant cries and her quivering cunt were all the signs he needed. He gritted his teeth and worked his hand underneath her. It was time to shove them both off that cliff to bliss.

Tucker caressed the tight bundle of nerves and Maggie hissed and jerked in response. Perfect. He then pinched it between his thumb and forefinger. "Come, baby. Give it to me now!" He lifted on his toes and changed the angle of his last thrust.

"Masterrrrr!" she screamed, the sound shattering every last thought in his head.

He pounded into her, his brain cells frying as he did. One last earth shattering scream from Maggie and he lost it. His cock jerked and everything he'd been holding back jetted into the woman he loved more than life.

Had anything in his life ever been this good? How could he possibly live without her? Tucker panted for breath as he tried to regain his equilibrium. Aftershocks from Maggie rippled across his cock, extending his pleasure beyond all expectations. He wanted to collapse. Fortunately, her muffled cries drew his attention and he realized he needed to move her position before it became painful. He pulled the knot at her wrist loose and gingerly lowered her arms to her sides. Her shoulders and arms would need a thorough massage before she tried to use them.

"Be still a minute longer and I'll help you."

He yanked the thong still mangled around her legs free and then pulled her back to his chest. A low moan escape her and he knew exactly how she felt. He'd used her hard and she'd sucked him dry. They'd both need a nap before they could even think about dinner. He carried her into the bedroom and laid her out on their bed. The rosy, satisfied flush of her body made his heart ache. She probably didn't realize just how much she'd saved him by coming into his life when she did. He, Mason and Levi had done the best they could at the time, not fully realizing what the long term affects might be.

He brushed his fingers across her face. Her eyes flickered several times before the finally opened and her tired gaze met his. To his surprise, the very male part of his body stirred at the sight. This is what her submission did to him. Or maybe it was simply the woman. There were many more facets to her and some he'd yet to discover.

"Now are you going to tell me what's going on?"

His shoulders sagged a fraction. The woman was sharp as a tack. "We should eat something first."

Maggie sat up and pulled herself across the bed to him. "You may have just blown the top of my head but that doesn't change the fact I knew something was up the minute I walked in. Now, are you going to tell me or do I have to do something drastic to get it out of you?"

He raised an eyebrow and contemplated what her idea of drastic might be. As much as he wanted to keep this light, the old sense of dread encroached. "Okay, then. At least let me grab a bottle of water for you and then we'll talk."

Tucker strode from the room, grabbed his pants on the way, and got dressed. Time to brace for the storm.

NINE

Levi swung the sledgehammer and drove it through the kitchen wall. He had big plans for designing a large open living space in his old house and the first thing he wanted to attack was the kitchen. He'd drawn up the plans for the amazing gourmet space yesterday and now he needed some good old-fashioned sweat equity to get his mind off a certain stubborn submissive.

It had been two days since the incident in Purgatory. Levi snorted at the thought. Yeah it had been an incident all right. Catori had driven him insane to the point he'd nearly taken her against a wall in a public space. Not that he hadn't done something like that in the past, but it wasn't how he imagined his first time with her. For the first time in his life he wanted to earn someone's trust before they got swept into a D/s relationship. He wanted what happened between them to be more than simply sex in a negotiated scene.

Levi paused in mid swing. What had happened to him? More exactly how had it happened so quickly? He smiled and drove the tool solidly through a chunk of drywall.

He was certain he'd left a lasting impression on Catori and tonight he'd make another move. A couple of days was more than enough time for her to stew on everything that worried her. The underlying, near dormant need he'd discovered had awakened and he'd learned from experience that once awakened it was damned near impossible to deny. Of course his plan to poke it again would work in his favor. He pondered the many ways he could challenge her. He'd seen enough of the stubborn sass that propelled her every day to know that an almost dare would get inside the armor she wore like a second set of clothes.

Except that her story the other night had thrown him for a loop. She'd discovered her submissive needs at a very young age and something about that didn't quite compute. She'd only shared half the story, he'd bet his life on that. They were both walking a fine line it seemed. She had secrets she didn't want to share as did he. How far could they go before someone broke?

His muscles strained from the physical effort it took to work through his task. Damn, it felt good to work like this again. These days he rarely went more than a few days without pushing his body through some kind of physical challenge to obliterate his ability to think too hard. He swung again, this time with double the force, and his sledgehammer went through not only some plaster and insulation, but straight into a stud as well.

"Shit."

"I may not be an expert, but I don't think that's the proper way to tear down a wall."

Levi whirled at the familiar voice and came face to face with Mason. Like a blast from the past his friend dominated the room with his ridiculous size. Same dark hair, same broad chest that used to be hell on the football field, and the exact same scowl he'd worn the last time they'd been together.

"You're right. You're not an expert."

Mason lifted his hand and covered his heart. "Ouch."

Levi rolled his eyes. "I wondered how long it would take for you to find out."

Mason scoffed. "Are you serious? I probably knew you were in town before you did."

Levi raised his arm and wiped the sweat dripping in his eyes. "I reckon you're probably right." Strangers stood out around here like an orange vest during hunting season.

"Probably? With the mouth of the south on the case, there likely isn't anyone left in town who doesn't know you're here."

"Yeah, I didn't exactly get the reception I thought I would." And he didn't want to think about how much that bothered him.

"Don't be too hard on her. You've been gone a long time. Seeing you is like meeting a long lost stranger who knows all about the skeletons living deep in the dark recess of her closet."

Levi closed his eyes and sucked in a ragged breath. Leave it to Mason to send them hurtling back all those years in an instant. He found himself back in the living room of Tucker's enormous house confronting the one man who'd pulled the proverbial rug out from under them. One minute they were declaring war against the most revered religious figurehead in the state and the next Nina stood before them covered in blood. So much blood. He squeezed his eyes tighter and grit his teeth against the memories. Hell waited for him every time he shut his eyes, he didn't need a daytime reminder as well.

"Don't do that, Mason. It's not fair."

"Neither were you, showing up out of the middle of nowhere. You go off and on the radar for years playing a stupid cat and mouse game. You don't respond to messages no matter how many I send. And now after all these years, you just ride into town and expect what? A family reunion? You know we can't afford that kind of exposure. What kind of punk ass selfish move are you playing here?" Mason's scowl deepened and Levi itched to beat it off his face. The tension between him and Mason had been building for years. His cold delivery of extremely healthy financial reports and his constant demand to know his whereabouts at all times had driven him incommunicado more than once over the years. Sometimes, he disappeared simply because he knew it would make Mason nuts, but most of the time he simply fought tumbling into a pit he couldn't climb back out of.

"If nothing has changed then why are you here? If you still want to hide our connection, then why come here? You certainly weren't invited. And if we're so close to exposure then why is Tucker traipsing up and down the eastern seaboard with a woman who trips into scandal every day on her way to work? Is that what you call a low profile?" Levi turned back to his task and kicked away a large chunk of drywall still clinging to the bare studs. Fuck Mason and the horse he rode in on.

"Contrary to popular belief, none of you pay attention to a word I say, Tucker included. Don't think I haven't been working my ass off on damage control."

Levi snorted. "Is there really that much risk after all this time? Why would anyone care about us or him anymore?" He didn't need to define "him" to Mason. He doubted anyone spoke his name out loud anymore. "Tucker deserves whatever happiness his new submissive brings him, but he isn't the only one."

"You have a sub in your pocket I don't know about?"

"Har har." Levi didn't really feel like laughing, his muscles flexed and the itch to return to work and save his temper gnawed at the edge of his mind. This conversation had already gone to shit and was only going to get worse. "You don't know anything about me. I came home because after a decade of wandering this is the only home I know. If you can't understand that then you have the issue not me. " Levi spun on his heels and faced Mason again. " And whether I have a submissive in my life is my business, not yours."

Mason arched his brow and studied him for a minute. "No. No way. Cannot happen. I heard about you and Tori in the club the other night. Pick someone else. Anyone else. She is not for you."

Levi ground his teeth together and tried to ignore Mason's annoying attitude. He wanted to tell him that he had no intention of picking someone else. From the moment he met Catori Ford he wanted nothing between them but skin. He ached to explore her both mentally and physically and he wasn't about to let someone who in all intents and purposes was a stranger to tell him who and what he did. "Don't go there again, Mace. You're way out of bounds. I don't want to kick you out of my house, but will if you keep crossing the line."

Mason scowled. "Seriously, Levi. You need to heed my warning on this one. There are a lot of beautiful submissives to choose from at Purgatory, all of them sure about what they want. Tori isn't one of them. She's confused about where she belongs and isn't ready for the likes of any of us. Hell, she isn't even sure whether she's Dominant or submissive. "

"She's submissive. That act Gabe has her performing at Purgatory is a God damned insult."

"Either way, she's trouble you don't want to fuck with. Trust me on this."

Levi compressed his lips in a tight line. What the hell was going on here? "What are you not saying? Do you have some *thing* going on with her I need to know about?

Just spit it out already."

"No, I do not have a *thing* with Tori. I've never spoken to her. That is Gabe's department." His scowl deepened. "That doesn't mean I don't know every aspect of the club and what goes on there. We may be absentee owners of Purgatory, but I've kept close tabs and all of our employees are carefully screened. A woman like her is complicated. She has a child. Did you know that?"

He shrugged. "Yeah, I've already met her. Actually met her before the mother. She was watching the counter at Nina's when I arrived and she has a way of wrapping you around her finger. I got hooked the minute she told me to grab a menu and join her at the counter for some coloring."

A low whistle sounded from Mason. "Are you falling for the mother or the daughter? Jesus, man. You need to run as fast as you can now from this mess before it's too late."

He gawked at his friend. His warnings made no sense. When had he become so cynical? "What happened to you? You sound cold and heartless."

Mason's features changed. His scowl disappeared and the crease in his forehead smoothed out. All outward signs of emotion evaporated before his eyes. "I do what has to be done to keep everyone safe, comfortable and worry free. You think coming back here is some cure for whatever baggage you're carrying around when it's the fucking source. Mark my words. You've just tripled every problem you've ever had by returning. This house is not going to slay your dragons. It's just a pile of brick and mortar that means nothing. The memories and home you want to claim are all in your head. Don't the Marines have a saying for this? Suck it up already and move on."

Anger boiled through Levi's brains. He'd tried to refrain from unleashing a decade's worth of shit on Mason and he'd done everything in his power to cut him to the bone. Fucker needed to be put in his place. He closed the distance between then in two strides with his fists clenched at his sides.

"Uhm... Hello?"

Both men whipped their heads around to find the woman in question standing in the open doorway gawking at them.

"I knocked but I guess you didn't hear me." She shifted from foot to foot looking ready to bolt in an instant.

Levi shot Mason a hard glance before turning his back on him. He moved toward Tori. "No problem. Mason and I are done here."

"Levi," Mason started.

"No, really. I've heard more than enough today." He kept his eyes on the woman in front of him, but the tension from Mason filled the space behind him. Despite that, the closer he drew to her the more his anger dissipated. She'd come to him.

"Okay I get the message, I'm going. But Levi, this isn't over," Mason warned moments before he walked out the still open front door.

"I really didn't mean to interrupt. You left this at my house the other night." She held up his favorite leather jacket that he'd forgotten all about. "Thought you might need it for when you rode your bike."

"I could have come and got it." He took it from her and laid it on the back of a nearby chair. "And don't worry about Mason. He has a flair for the dramatic."

"If you say so." She bit her lip before she continued. "I didn't know how to contact you and neither did Nina. So she told me how to find you here." She glanced around the mess of what used to be the small living room that would now become part of the giant open concept living and kitchen area. "I like what you've done with the place. Very uhm... Industrial."

"I know. It's a big fucking mess. But trust me when it's done, all this will be worth it."

"Is that the plans for what you're doing there?" She pointed to the architectural drawings he'd done up the day before and taped to the one wall in this room that wouldn't get torn down.

"Yup. I have a vision."

She walked over to the paper and studied them without saying a word. He studied her. A tank top and short pants clung to the body he ached to explore. He preferred the short shorts from the other night or better yet the skirt she'd worn to Purgatory. The shorts showed off her long legs to perfection but the skirt gave him access to her sexy thong and what lay beneath it. He started to sweat again. For that five minutes he'd fingered her heat or the thirty seconds he'd savored her taste, he'd had two fitful nights of sleep and two very long days of work filled with nothing but his Catori.

Yeah. His. Even if she didn't know it yet.

"Oh my God. This is all going to fit in here?"

He walked up behind her and looked over her shoulder. "For the most part. I am contemplating expanding the kitchen wall out here," he pointed to the far outside wall, "and making the whole room even larger."

"That's going to be a dream kitchen." Her voice sounded wistful when she said it.

"I hope so." He'd thought of her the entire time he planned it out. He brought his left hand to the wall on the other side of her head and caged her in. "Is that why you came here? To talk about kitchens? Or have you made up your mind?" He nudged her hair to the side and scraped his teeth along the column of her neck. Something he'd fantasized about for two days non-stop.

Her head fell back on his chest and lolled to the side, giving him better access to her neck. "I still don't know what to do. I hate complicated and trust me, my life is already more complex than I need."

He bit down as she uttered the last, which she quickly followed up with a quiet moan. "What we do does not have to be complicated. In fact, in my experience, it can often be a freeing experience that reduces stress."

When she didn't respond, he could imagine the thousand reasons why she couldn't be with him like this running through her mind. "Stop thinking about it so hard and go with your gut. Sometimes logic is overrated."

"I have Hannah to consider. It makes something like this more complicated."

"Why? Do you think I require submission twenty-four/seven from you?"

She spun in his arms and studied him intently. "Don't you?"

"No." He leaned forward and kissed her, letting his answer sink in. Levi took his time exploring her mouth without the fierce need to dominate pushing through. Her mouth opened like a flower in the bright morning sunshine, slow and lazy but eager as hell.

"Not every moment between us has to be about submission. We had lives before we met and we'll continue to have those same lives while we're together."

"I don't want to get lost again." She spoke the words so quietly he barely heard them.

He pulled back and stared into her eyes. They were full of so many emotions he couldn't tell one from the other long enough to gauge what was going on in her mind. "Is that what happened before?"

She blinked and whatever had been there disappeared. Her mind withdrew and she pulled out of his arms. "It's ancient history, Levi. I answered you honestly last night, but I refuse to keep going back there. I think I should go. I'm going to be late picking up Hannah from her playdate. I'll call you."

In the blink of an eye, she'd shut down and he'd lost this round. Dammit. Part of him wanted to stop her and the other knew she'd make the right decision the less he pushed. He shoved his hands in his pockets and watched her walk through his front door much the way Mason did not long before her. The summer breeze lifted her hair and he found himself transfixed by the image she presented when running away. No, he wasn't going to stop her this time, but any last lingering doubts he might have harbored evaporated. He *had* to have her.

He moved to the window and watched her climb into that ridiculous bright yellow bug of hers and crank the engine. She looked up and their gazes met. For a second he hoped she'd climb back out and admit she'd made a mistake. Instead, she turned away from him, backed out of his gravel drive way and drove away. He watched her go until her taillights disappeared in the distance.

She said she'd call. How long would it take before she remembered she still didn't have his phone number? And what the hell was a playdate?

TEN

"You ignored my advice and went out there didn't you?" Josie, her life long best friend, tossed her keys into the bowl on the small foyer table and slammed the door shut. She stared through Tori as if she were a piece of transparent glass. "Girl, he is going to chew you up and spit you out. At least that's the impression I got from what you told me. Is that something you're prepared to go through again?"

Tori blew at the hair hanging in her face and turned away from her friend. "I don't see why you're making a big deal out of this. He left his jacket here and since I couldn't call him to let him know, I rode out to his house yesterday and gave it to him. It was a nice gesture."

"Nice gesture my ass. Handing him that leather jacket was the equivalent of waving a red flag in front of a bull that says 'Come and get me, I'm ready to get tied down and fucked hard.'"

"Josie! Hannah is right down the hall," she whispered harshly.

"I can hear her singing, which means she's got her headphones on and can't hear a thing. Now don't try to use your child to avoid talking about this. So what happened? I want every detail." Her friend took a seat at one of the stools across the island from where she worked.

"Nothing much. He wasn't alone when I got there and I think I interrupted something important. They were both pissed and about to come to blows when I barged in."

Tori took out her rolling pin and began rolling the fresh made dough across her floured countertops. One of the smartest things she'd done when she moved into this old house was this island and its quartz countertop. She loved that she could do all of her baking and prep directly on the wide surface. It made assembly line pies not only possible, but enjoyable.

"They? As in another woman? That sounds juicy. Who was it?"

She shrugged. "She was a he and I think his name was Mason." No way did Josie need to know that the Mason she spoke of was another Dom she'd seen on occasion at Purgatory and many times at the Fire and Ice restaurant, which happened to cater to many of the clientele from Purgatory. Until this morning she'd only thought of him as some obvious rich guy who didn't socialize much. She'd never seen him with a submissive and he always wore a scowl on his face that made him look permanently pissed.

"Hmm. Is he a walking, talking wet dream bad boy like Levi?" Josie's eyes had glazed over as if she was picturing Levi or Mason or both.

Tori frowned. "Only if uptight gorgeous in a business suit is your type. Otherwise, you're out of luck."

Josie wrinkled her nose. "Seriously?"

She nodded.

"Dammit. That's so disappointing. I was hoping Levi had a hot friend I could borrow for a few days."

"I thought you said Levi was bad news and I should avoid him at all costs."

Her friend grabbed a fresh sliced peach and popped it into her mouth. "I said you should avoid him and his type.

You aren't equipped to handle that kind of volatility."

"Oh thanks. So now I'm stupid and a simpering female with no backbone or ability to have fun with a sexy man without going too far."

"Puhleeze. You know that's not what I meant. What happened to your plan to wait until you were ready and then find and settle down with a boring business man with a boring job he's had for at least ten years after you've thoroughly checked out his mental health."

Tori's mouth dropped open at her friend's assessment. Is that what she sounded like? "I never said boring. I said stable. S. T. A. B. L. E. Big difference. I thought of all people you'd understood that." She lowered her voice to barely a whisper. "I cannot go through another ordeal like I did with Bill." Not long after Hannah's birth, her father had started to change. Little things at first, until he started questioning her every move. The paranoia had escalated from there.

Josie rolled her eyes. "You say stable, I say boring. Tomato, tah mah toe. Whatever. The point is you don't pick out a lover like you're ordering sushi at the deli. There is destiny and fate you have to deal with. Not to mention some little sexual quirks you're not likely to find in your ideal *stable* man. It also doesn't mean you should jump on the first bad boy to cuff you to a wall either."

Tori pulled the first pie plate closer and spread the dough in the bottom. "You make me regret telling you my secrets."

"Aww, Tori. Don't be like that. I'm looking out for you. I don't want you to settle for some poor schmuck who will bore you to death, but jumping on the back of the first stud muffin's bike for some kinky sex is a sure path to heartbreak for you." She plucked another peach from the pile and swallowed it whole. "Now, me on the other hand. I live for the three night stand guys like Levi."

"Three nights?"

"Yeah, when the sex is so good one night is not enough so you extend the wild monkey sex to three sessions. Long enough to get it out of your system and short enough to not let any of those pesky emotions get in the way."

Tori pondered Josie's latest sexual revelation as she piled peaches into a big bowl and mixed the flour, sugar and vanilla to make the perfect filling. She envied her friend and the ease with which she went out and scratched her itch without batting an eye when she was done.

Could the three-night stand be the perfect solution to her dilemma? Levi had made it pretty clear that he planned to pursue her and despite her head telling her what a bad idea it would be, her body clamored for her to say yes. Back at his house with his body pressed to hers she'd been that close to giving in. There was no longer a doubt in her mind what she wanted, but was she brave enough to take it?

One by one she filled each pie pan with the peach mixture before adding the secret ingredient her grandmother had taught her. Each one would have the perfect blend of thick and creamy consistency to satisfy any pie lover. If Levi had been impressed before, wait until he got one of these bad babies fresh out of the oven.

"Why are you making so many peach pies anyway? Did you get a special order?"

"Uhm... No."

Josie groaned and dropped her head onto the worktop with a thud. "Don't tell me," she spoke into her folded arms. "Peach pie is Levi's favorite."

"That doesn't matter. The peaches were fresh at the farmer's market today so I grabbed them at a great price. Plus I dug out my grandmother's favorite recipe for a little change of pace. These are going to go over great."

"Oh. My. God. It's worse than I thought. You need

an intervention already."

"Shut up. I do not. Besides, I ran out on him like I was at the gates of hell being chased by the devil himself. He's probably thinking he saved himself from one big hassle right about now."

"Noooooo," her friend cried. "Stop talking. I can't take anymore." She lifted her head. "Have I taught you nothing? We talked about this. Hard to get, not crazy lunatic. No down on your luck and certainly no talk EVER about men from the past."

Tori cringed.

"No, Tori. Please please please tell me you didn't."

She wisely kept her mouth shut. Josie was on a tear now and it was best to let her finish the rant and get it over with.

"Although in this case, it's probably for the best. Hopefully everything you said scared him off and he won't be back."

The phone rang and interrupted the rest of Josie's rant. Their gazes met and they both broke out into laughter.

"It can't be," Tori said.

"I'm saying a prayer."

Tori wiped her hands and grabbed her cell from the counter. "It's not him." She depressed the talk button. "Hi, Nana."

"Ooh ooh say hi to Nana for me."

"Josie says hi."

"Hi back to her, hon. It feels like ages since I've seen her. You too."

"I know, Nana. We've been so busy and now that Hannah is out of pre-school there's been no extra time. She keeps me on my toes day and night."

"Good. Then you won't mind if I come and get her for a few days."

"What?"

"Don't sound so shocked, Catori. You know I've been dying to spend more time with my great granddaughter. I won't be around forever and I want to take advantage of every moment I have left."

Tori sighed. Leave it to her Nana to use a little guilt to get what she wanted. "Oh please, you're as healthy as a horse. You aren't going anywhere."

"You say that now, but no one really knows. So I can expect you to drop her off on your way to work tonight?"

Tori laughed as what little resistance she had crumbled. "You know I will. I have the dinner shift so I'll bring her by around four thirty."

Her Nana squealed, the sound squeezing Tori's heart. They were way overdue for a nice long visit.

"You are a good girl, Catori. I'll see you in a few hours." With that her grandmother clicked off. Tori put her phone back on the counter and turned to her friend.

"That woman is nuts. Trying to tell me that she needs to see Hannah because she might not be around much longer." Tori shook her head and went back to filling pies. The call had made her realize how little time she had left before she had to get ready for work. Tonight would be a very busy night at the restaurant, Fridays always were, and she didn't want to be late.

"No, Tori. That woman is a genius. She just gave you some much needed time off from motherhood. Now what are you going to do with it?"

She looked up at her friend, her hand pausing in mid air.

"Tori," Josie whined. "You are really killing me here. You've just been given several days of freedom and it didn't even cross your mind what you could do with it?"

"Sleep?" she offered.

Josie narrowed her eyes.

She looked down and tried to hide her smile. She didn't want to give her friend any more ammunition to use against her in the conversation. Tori's head may not have gotten on board with the idea yet, but her body certainly did. The ache between her legs and the erect nipples pushing against her bra sent the message loud and clear.

Three night stand.

ELEVEN

Tori rushed through the back entrance of Fire and Ice at full speed. Her trip out to Nana's to drop off Hannah had taken a lot longer than she'd expected. Her child of course had no problem with the opportunity to spend time with her great grandmother but the minute Tori had pulled out a peach pie for Nana and Hannah to share, her child had launched into the whole story about meeting a man named Levi who loved peach pie and had tattoos on his arms like her mama's.

The minute Nana's eyebrows had risen, Tori knew she'd be late for work. She danced around the conversation without ever saying much until finally she'd begged off with the excuse of being late for work.

"Tori, there you are!" Julia, one of the other hostesses, exclaimed. "Gabe's in the dining area searching for you."

Tori shoved her legs into the small black skirt of her uniform and wiggled it over her hips. "Shit. Of course the one time I'm late he notices."

"I'll let him know you're in the bathroom and buy you an extra few minutes to finish dressing."

She grabbed the purple blouse from her locker.

"Thanks. I'll be out in a sec." In a hurry, she buttoned the blouse and then grabbed the heels that were also part of the uniform. Four inches of heels made her almost six-foot frame tower over a lot of customers but Gabe insisted that the shoes were necessary. He often told her that standing out in this crowd wasn't a bad thing.

With one last glance in the mirror to ensure she'd meet Gabe's approval, Tori ran from the room and ended up face first into Gabe's chest on the other side of the door. He grabbed her arms to keep her from falling.

"Whoa. Where's the fire?"

Tori looked into the warm hazel eyes of her boss with relief when she realized he wasn't upset with her. "Sorry, I heard you were looking for me and I didn't want to keep you waiting."

"You were late tonight. Is everything okay? How is Hannah?" His look of genuine concerned touched her.

"Hannah is great. I just had to take her out to my grandmother's house. She called today insisting that it was time for my daughter to come for an extended visit and you know how Nanas can be."

Gabe threw back his head and laughed. "Oh yes I do. So I'll forgive you for being late but you owe me one and I'm about to call in that favor."

The troubled look on his face made her more than a little wary. Dare she ask? What the hell? "Sure, whatever you need, I'm there."

"One of the private dining rooms was booked at the last minute tonight and I'm short a waitress. I could use your help."

Tori heaved a sigh of relief. "Is that it? Geez, Gabe. You were making me nervous enough I expected something far worse."

"Don't go forgiving me yet. You haven't seen the work involved."

She half heard Gabe's statement as she moved around the work station, where she grabbed a small order tray and a few supplies she thought she might need to take care of a private party.

"Will the bar be open in the room?" If she needed to work with a bartender she wanted to make sure he had everything he needed.

"It's open but the customer prefers to only have one server. He's asked for complete privacy and I'm in the position of making sure he gets what he needs."

"Of course. The customers always come first and the customer is always right."

Gabe grabbed her arm and halted her movements. "Not always, Tori. Sometimes even the waitress gets too uncomfortable with what goes on in a private party. If that becomes the case then you are highly encouraged to come and find me."

"I'm sure that won't be necessary. I'm not a wilting flower and there isn't much I haven't already seen at least once."

"Tori, stop." Gabe's voice lowered an octave and she immediately recognized it for what it was. The command of a Dom.

She turned to look at him, thoroughly confused.

"I need you to know you have options and I expect you to acknowledge what I'm saying. Do you understand that if anything goes wrong in there you can either leave or use the club safeword to make things stop?"

"Gabe, what the hell? I'm serving dinner in the restaurant, not working the VIP lounge in Purgatory. Why in the world would I need a safeword for something like that?"

He narrowed his eyes and gave her a stern look of disapproval. Tori bit her lip at the power she felt emanating from him. Every ounce of the Dom had come to life and turned all its attention to her. Part of her brain knew she needed to ask questions or argue with him, but the stronger part of her wanted to comply. "Yes, Sir, I understand," she replied.

"Good girl. Now hurry up and get in there. Some guests do not like to be kept waiting." At that, he turned and disappeared so fast she remained transfixed staring after him. It wasn't like him to be this protective or this stern with her when she'd done nothing wrong. Something bothered him.

Tori shook her mind clear. Whatever it was it would have to wait. She had a job to do and time was ticking. She grabbed the last of her supplies and headed to private dining room number two. When she passed by the restaurant restroom, she wistfully glanced over at the door. Stress over Gabe's strange behavior had made her break out in a sweat. The idea of taking a few minutes to splash some cold water on her face sounded suddenly like heaven.

Instead she went to the door two past the bathroom and pushed through the unlocked door. The lights were dim but not dark, just enough to give the room a sensual ambience. The room was one of the larger private spaces but it had been cleared of all furniture except for one large dining table in the middle of the room and the built-in bar that ran along the back wall.

Rich, gold color on the walls and the dark wood tray ceiling gave off an intimate vibe as much as it spoke to the money that flowed through this room. The lone hexagon table had been set for only two diners. She quickly assessed the table settings and linens to see if she needed more supplies. Satisfied that the preparations were adequate she headed over to the bar to ensure everything had been fully stocked. She wanted to be prepared for whatever the customers may require.

She moved quickly and efficiently and it was only

after she'd set up everything the way she wanted that she took a moment to look to the wall of windows she knew overlooked the sparkling city skyline. Her heart stuttered at the man who stood looking out.

Holy hell. How had she missed him?

"I'm sorry, Sir. I didn't see you there. Is there anything I can get you at this time? As soon as your guest arrives we can start the dinner service if you'd like. Whatever pleases you." Even in the semi darkness of the window alcove she made out some of the details of her charge tonight. Black dress shirt and black pants perfectly tailored to fit his tall, lanky frame. Probably another rich Dom who reveled in high protocols and perfect submissives. Something she'd never be.

The shadowy figure turned and stepped into a shaft of light coming from one of the overhead chandeliers. She gasped. "Levi?"

"In the flesh," he drawled.

"I don't understand. What's going on? Are you meeting someone here?" And why did her stomach now cramp at the thought of him entertaining another woman? No, not just another woman. Probably a submissive. These rooms were strictly available to Purgatory members only.

"I am meeting someone," He strode forward and she admired everything about him as he did. Messy dark hair sort of combed into place but still with that attractive I just rolled out of bed look. His arms were covered so she couldn't admire those sexy ass tattoos of his, but it didn't escape her notice the way the fabric of his shirt tightened across his chest as he moved. To her surprise, he didn't stop until he was well inside her personal space. "And I'm really glad she's finally here."

"Huh?" *Ohhh.* "You set this up?"

"What can I say?" He reached forward, lifted her chin and pressed a light kiss to her mouth. A firm yet amazingly gentle touch. Soft. A little like velvet. "I'm an impatient man and I wanted to see you again."

Tori's chest tightened. What was she supposed to say to that?

"It seems every time we meet we get interrupted before we finish our conversation. I figured coming here and booking you as my waitress for the night gave me a pretty good shot at finally getting you to myself." He covered her mouth with his and thoroughly devoured her with a kiss that had to have been designed to melt her brain. She opened against his onslaught and his tongue delved inside her mouth. *Holy shit.*

A moment later, he stepped back and she lifted her hand to her lips and traced the area where he'd kissed. She had a feeling the impression would last forever. The man was far more potent than he had the right to be.

"So that's why Gabe was acting so weird. He expects me to be pissed about this." She walked over to the bar and sat down on one of the stools, crossing one leg over the other. "Why exactly is that? I realize I butted in the other night where I shouldn't have at the club, but since you've decided to orchestrate our first date without telling me, then I think the least you could do is give me an explanation."

A gorgeous smile crossed Levi's face and Tori tried to ignore the pack of butterflies trying to take flight in her stomach. He closed the space between them and took a seat next to her. "Fair enough. We should talk first anyway."

"First?" She held her breath half excited about and half dreading what he might say next.

He leaned forward until she felt the warm puff of his breath against her ear when he spoke. "First we talk, then we fuck."

Tori's heart slammed inside her chest. Holy hell. His crude, but very direct statement took her by surprise. The

Dom she'd glimpsed the other night had returned in full force. She tried to catch her breath while waiting for the outrage that had to be coming. No such luck. Her nipples tightened and pushed against the lace of her bra and her sex squeezed at the mere thought of having him inside her.

Oh God. She couldn't breathe for thinking about it.

"Relax, Catori. I fully intend for everything between us to be one hundred percent consensual. That's why we're here."

Thoughts tumbled through her mind one right after the other with none making a lick of sense. "I should find out what you want to eat."

His eyebrow quirked and the sudden image of his head between her legs flashed through her mind. It wasn't the first time she imagined the scrape of his beard against her soft skin and she doubted it would be the last.

"I mean I need to place your dinner order with the staff. I still have a job to fulfill."

"Already done." He glanced at his watch. "Dinner should arrive in about fifteen minutes. Long enough for us to chat over a glass of wine. Your only job is to relax and enjoy a night off."

"But--"

"Catori." His use of her full name complete with a warning tone made his intent clear. She pulled her bottom lip between her teeth.

Apparently satisfied she'd stopped arguing, Levi stood up and walked behind the bar. "Do you have a preference?"

She shook her head. Her tongue felt three times its normal size and she didn't think she could string words together quite yet.

While he poured two glasses of red wine, she watched his movements. His long tanned fingers moved with incredible efficiency. There were calluses and small white scar lines here and there, making it clear he'd spent a fair amount of time doing manual labor. But at what? She knew so little about him. He pushed one of the goblets across the bar to her. "Shall we make a toast?"

"O-okay," she stammered and picked up her glass.

He lifted his glass and held it out to her. "To discovering and satisfying long dormant needs." He clinked his glass to hers and she sat mute, wondering what the hell to say. She gulped her wine and thanked the Gods for the perfect drink at the perfect time.

"I don't get this," she blurted. "I mean why me?"

Levi slowly came around the bar with a thoughtful expression across his face and settled on the stool next to her before he answered. "Because you're beautiful and vital. You're smart and sweet and make the best damn peach pie I've ever tasted. That is more important than you think." He winked at her, making her blush from head to toe. "You have curves that don't quit and I can't remember feeling this strong of an attraction ever. From the moment we met I wanted to get to this. You and I alone. But the night at the club sealed the deal as far as I'm concerned. You were already half way to perfect until I realized there was a sweet responsive submissive waiting to be discovered."

"You give me way more credit than I deserve. I *was* submissive. As in past tense. I put that all behind me many years ago." She grabbed her glass and took another large swallow of wine. "I have a different life now."

"I don't actually believe that, though. Hard to accept you've put it behind you when you work in the only BDSM club in town. You may not be actively participating like you used to, but you're far from leaving it all behind. At the moment you're living vicariously and I aim to change that."

She shrugged. "When you have a child to take care of you do what you have to. I'm familiar with lifestyle protocols and working here pays very well, so it was a no brainer when I needed cash. Don't read more into it than is really there."

He studied her for a moment before he spoke, "Fair enough." But she could tell from the look on his face he didn't really believe her. "I take it Hannah's father wasn't a Dom."

Tori choked on the wine she sipped and barely managed to keep the liquid from spewing out of her mouth. She grabbed a napkin and dabbed at her lips. "Uhm, no Hannah's father is definitely not a Dom. One hundred percent vanilla all the way. Almost a prude, as a matter of fact."

Levi's eyebrow quirked. "So you set your submission aside for love then?"

"Not exactly."

He grabbed her wrists and wrapped his hands firmly around them, drawing her closer. "We can't talk in circles here, Catori." His voice lowered and brooked no argument. "What's going to happen between us requires trust and honesty. That means I need to know what happened to change your mind about submission. I don't want to accidentally trigger a negative reaction."

It was clear she wasn't going to get out of telling him everything. Not everything though. She couldn't handle a repeat of the last time she decided to be completely honest. What a joke. No one ever really wanted all the good and the bad. They wanted the best of what she had to offer and then a sliver of reality that wouldn't offend anyone's sensibilities. The truth meant packing up and moving somewhere new to start all over again.

"It had nothing to do with love," she admitted. "I put it behind me out of pain and not the good kind of pain."

"Pain. Hmm," his voice vibrated with sensuality. "Well, we can certainly get to the good kind. After you tell me why."

She sighed. "Fine. But don't say I didn't warn you because the truth is a real buzzkill."

"I can handle it."

"I was seventeen when I was introduced to BDSM by my first boyfriend. He was a few years older and far more worldly than I ever hoped to be," she tried to keep the wistful tone out of her voice and failed. The past hurt, but it also contained many of the best moments of her life. "I know what you're thinking. That's too young. That I was taken advantage of. Or a million variations of the same objections. But you're wrong. That relationship was intense, and exciting, and more than I ever could have hoped for. Seth was simply the Dom of my dreams." Memories flooded through her mind as she spoke, taking root and digging in. She hadn't dared think of him in more than fleeting moments for so very long. Except when she slept. Seth always came to her when she least expected him.

"Go on."

Tori tried to read Levi's reactions and failed. He appeared patient and interested. Except for the underlying tension she detected every so often in the flex of his muscles.

"After I turned eighteen and graduated from high school, we decided to go a little more public with our relationship. We told our parents we were dating and we even ventured out to our first BDSM club play party. I thought life was perfect." The pit in her stomach sank like a lead balloon. She'd been so damned naive back then. Love and submission completely blinded her to the harsh details of reality.

"So what happened? Things didn't work out? Did you get hurt?"

The familiar burn of tears at the back of her eyes grabbed her concentration as she fought to not let them drop. "Not in the way you're probably thinking. When our relationship began Seth had already joined the Army, shortly after we got together he began coming home every weekend. A few days after we got engaged, he was sent to Afghanistan." Having not spoken the words aloud in a very long time made talking about it so much worse. "Three months later and two days before my nineteenth birthday, Seth was killed in action."

"Shit." Levi pulled her from her stool and wrapped his arms around her. "I had no idea. I'm so sorry."

"Don't be. I knew if I ever wanted to be with another man I would have to tell them eventually and in your case--sooner."

Levi drew back and stared into her eyes. "Are you telling me there's been no one since Hannah's father?"

She shook her head, embarrassment heating her cheeks and neck.

"How long, Catori?" She'd told him before, but the Dom in him couldn't resist hearing it again.

"Hannah's father has been gone two years, but it's been closer to three since I've been, uhm, intimate with a man. The break up was rough and even though I haven't heard a word from him in all this time, I haven't forgotten."

Levi's mouth dropped open for a second before he quickly clamped it closed. She inwardly cringed at the questions that must be racing through his mind. What was wrong with her that she couldn't lure her baby's father into bed? Or maybe why she hadn't already hooked up with someone at the club. She'd had more than her fair share of offers to dominate a variety of men and women for that matter. But until she walked out of Nina's kitchen and found the most rugged, magnetic man coloring along side her daughter, no one had sparked her interest even a little.

"There isn't anything wrong with me in case you were wondering," she blurted out before averting her eyes.

He grasped her chin and tilted her head until her

gaze met his. "That thought never entered my mind. I've already seen how well you respond to the right stimuli, remember?" His thumb began rubbing back and forth across her lips. "For example. I know you enjoy being restrained."

Since it wasn't a question, she keep her mouth firmly shut. The almost hypnotic touch of his skin against hers made her mind begin short circuiting. His touch alone managed to push her focus away from the past. Her pussy tingled and she fought not to squirm.

"What else do you like?" His request came out very casual and easy to go along with.

"This might sound silly, since it has nothing to do with sex." She hesitated. He'd probably think she sounded like an idiot.

"Go on."

Tori took a deep breath and went for it. "I loved sitting at his feet with his hand touching me in a soft caress." Especially when he ran his fingers through her hair. That sensation had actually been quite erotic to her. "I realize how mundane that must sound and I can't explain why..."

"It gave you a sense of security and peace. And it gives the Dom an unequivocal belief that the relationship is in perfect sync to see a submissive so settled. Don't ever be ashamed of any aspect of your submission. It goes well beyond simple sex for many people and it's disrespectful to find shame in that."

"That's not exactly what I meant."

"I know you didn't and I appreciate you sharing with me. Little things often mean the most." He caressed her bare shoulders, his warmth loosening some of her tight muscles. "Tell me more."

"Uhm...I don't know... I've never talked about this."

Levi thread his fingers through her hair, wrapped

his hand behind her neck and pulled her closer. "In here, in private or in the club there is nothing you can't say to me. There is also no such thing as too dirty or too slutty. So don't try to soften your descriptions or your needs. I demand you tell me exactly what you like and what you don't and feel free to use the dirtiest fucking words you can think of."

The heat that flared to life in his eyes matched the heat growing inside her. "Seth loved to cane me until I squealed like a pig and I like to come until I nearly pass out."

Her words incited Levi into action. With a handful of hair grasped in his hand he pulled her head back until he'd exposed her neck and she gasped from the sudden twinge of pain.

"You liked the cane?" He bit at her neck and Tori wanted to melt against him.

"I loved the marks it gave me for days. The constant reminder of the gifts my Dom gave me made each day special. But the flogger, now that's my favorite." A shiver ran through her at the memory. "The sensation of many tendrils slapping across my skin is like a thousand rough kisses all at the same time."

"What about toys?" Heat flooded her cheeks. He smiled. "I'm going to take that as a definite yes."

Tori dipped her head and tried to hide her gaze. This was far harder to discuss than she thought.

"Nope." He cupped her chin and pulled her head until their gazes met once again. "Eyes on me, Catori. Always on me."

She swallowed hard, unsure what to say next.

"I think that's enough talking for now. You have a safeword and I'll expect you to use it if you need to. If I do something that's too much then you'll tell me."

"Yes, Si-I mean Levi."

TWELVE

Levi waited for his brain to explode. That's what this woman did to him. From her honesty about her past to the details of what she loved about her submission made him so damn hard. At this point it was taking an enormous amount of restraint not to bend her over and bury himself inside her.

"Mmm. I can imagine you with many lovely marks my, Catori. Your olive skin tone must look captivating when it turns red. Which means tonight I will use my crop."

Tori moaned, the sound going straight to his cock. "Kneel, Catori. I prefer to hear the rest while you're on your knees."

To her credit, her hesitation only lasted a few heartbeats before she began to sink toward the floor. From the moment he'd discovered her in Purgatory he'd imagined this moment. It amazed him how much her submission meant to him.

"Knees a little further apart, please." He imagined or hoped he'd find her as wet and excited as he suspected. In this position, her spine went ramrod straight and her eyes cast downward. Apparently, for her, submission was much like riding a bike--you never forget how it's done.

He checked his watch and a knock sounded at the door. Perfect timing.

"Stay there while I have our dinner served." He half expected her to object, but she maintained position and didn't utter a word. She gave him the sense she was halfway to the zone every submissive sought. He definitely planned to get her there tonight and then some.

Levi moved quickly, anxious to get their scene underway. He took the dinner cart at the door and sent the server away. He'd take care of everything himself. While there'd likely come a time when he wanted to scene in public, tonight he had no desire for an audience.

When he got everything set up he returned to Tori and pulled her to her feet. "Have you used nipple clamps before?"

She nodded. "Yes."

"A limit for you?"

"No, Sir," she answered.

"I prefer, Levi. Every time I hear Sir I think someone is referring to my father and I have no intention of being anything at all like my father. With you, I'd love to hear the word Master fall from your lips, but to me it's a title that has to be earned. So until you're ready to call me Master, I'd prefer Levi. Understand?"

"Yes, Levi."

"Good girl." He reached for the first hook of her corset and began unfastening them. He took his time, building the anticipation for them both. He longed to see her breasts and fortunately they had plenty of time to get there. With each fastener he brushed his fingers along another section of her skin. Each touch elicited a gasp or a sigh that he felt clear to his toes. When he finished, he laid the corset across the bar top. Her large breasts hung heavy with rosy brown nipples tight, perfectly ready for the clamps he had in mind for her. He pinched each one before he reached underneath them and lifted them to his mouth. One after the other he laved the hard tips until she moaned in bliss. "How does that feel? Does your pussy ache?"

She nodded. "Yes."

"Perfect." He pulled the first clover clamp from his pocket and held it up for her to see. "I'm going to put these on you and then maybe watch you squirm through dinner. I'll enjoy every panting moment as you start to unravel in front of me."

"That sounds a little sadistic."

He laughed. "Does it? It sounds fucking perfect to me. The thought of you begging me to fuck you in the middle of a meal turns me the hell on."

"Cocky too," she responded, but the flare of excitement crossed her face before she could hide it.

He cupped her right breast first while watching her eyes the whole time. As much as he loved how she felt in his hands, he wanted to watch her reactions more.

After several rapid blinks, her gaze settled on his. He smiled. "You are beautiful in your submission, Catori."

"Thank you."

He flicked his thumbs across both nipples and watched her mouth drop open and form a gorgeous O. Her mouth fascinated him. Hell, everything about her fascinated him. Now to make her feel even better. He squeezed the clamp and slid it across one taut bud and released it, allowing the metal to slowly bite down.

"Okay?" he asked.

"Yes," she breathed, her voice ragged.

"Very good." He pulled the other clamp out. "Now for the other." Before she'd fully adjusted to the first, he attached the second device to her left breast and studied her eyes for reaction. Her pupils dilated and she ground her teeth against the pain. He'd leave them at this tension for now before he screwed them tighter.

"Just another few adjustments and we'll be ready to eat." Of course his mind would be on her pussy the entire meal. Wondering what she tasted like and how wet she'd get sitting across from him waiting for him to continue their scene. He grabbed the edges of her skirt and shimmied the snug material over her hips until the entire garment was bunched around her hips. He breathed deep at the sight of her--" He spun her around. *Thong. Damn.* The sight of that thin strip of fabric nestled between her ass cheeks made him crazy. He fingered that little piece of silk from top to bottom and back before slipping under the edge and curling his fingers around what basically amounted to a string. In one fast and rough movement, he tore her thong, the rip of flimsy fabric echoing around them.

"What are you thinking now?" he growled.

"I could have just taken it off for you," she teased.

He pulled her hips roughly toward him, lifted her to waist height. "Legs," he demanded. She got his drift and wrapped those luscious limbs around his back, leaving her pussy pressed against his dick. It was his turn to grit his teeth and continue with his plan. He carried her to the table and placed her on the chair he'd prepared. She whimpered in distress when he unwrapped her legs and forced her to comply. The resulting frown on her face made him smile. "Next time you want a reward you might think about holding that smart tongue."

An involuntary groan escaped her as she tried to keep her composure and failed. The moment her butt had hit the slim piece of wood for her to sit on she'd realized where he'd placed her. The bondage chair. Although most in the club affectionately called it the cross chair because it had arms built into the sides that could be extended so the submissive got her arms tied out to her sides. Her stomach trembled. As much as she hated the way he'd drag this out, she'd do just about anything at the moment for more. Her hesitation at entering into even a temporary situation where he dominated her was quickly fading. It had been so damn long since anyone had handled her like this. How could she have forgotten what this was like?

She looked into his eyes and nearly swallowed her tongue at the sight. Hungry lust stared back at her, making her stomach flip. He wanted her as much as she wanted him. Crap. This was about to get complicated.

Of course the constant pressure on her sensitized nipples had her strung tight with a constant arc of sensation running straight to her clit. She definitely wanted more of what he could give her, but if he didn't do something soon she might go out of her mind.

"Please," she mumbled.

"Sweet," he responded. "But not yet. Spread your legs."

Anxious for him to get on with it, she quickly did as he asked and placed her thighs on top of the supports. An immediate sense of vulnerability began to creep over her. He reached for the belts and strapped them on just above her knees. He did the same for the fasteners at her ankles. Her legs were now stretched open and she had no recourse to close them. He could pretty much do whatever he wanted. A little sliver of fear niggled at the back of her mind.

"Do you remember your safeword?" he asked.

Duh. How could she have forgotten? "Yes. Elvis."

He shook his head and continued. Levi lifted the arm supports from the back of the chair and placed them to her sides, perpendicular with the floor. From there he was able to strap her arms wide, leaving her completely immobile. Only her head remained free. Of course there were other options to restrain her one hundred percent if he so chose. She hoped not.

She held her breath and waited for what came next.

He stood back and stared at her as if admiring a piece of art or an object he desired. Her stomach fluttered and her pussy wept. Tears welled in her eyes.

The look on his face changed in an instant. "What's wrong? Too much? Dammit, Catori why aren't you using your safeword or at least telling me it's too much?" He stepped toward her and reached for the buckle across her right arm.

"No, don't," she whispered, her face heating at the husky tone of her voice.

"What?" He let go and knelt between her legs until their gazes met. "Tell me, beautiful. What's going on it that head of yours?"

Tori swallowed past the embarrassment and decided to be honest. "It's been so long. I didn't remember how I would feel to have someone look at me the way you do."

The worry crease across his forehead relaxed a fraction. "Oh. You're okay then?"

"More than okay. But can we get to the good stuff now?" she smiled wickedly, knowing that she was being a bit bratty but feeling desperate to break past the reservations still plaguing her.

"You like to hide your nerves and vulnerability behind a shield of sarcasm, don't you?"

She frowned at him. Part of her wanted to say something smart in return even though he might be a little bit right. "I mostly just wanted you to know it really was okay to keep going."

"Mostly?" He cupped her chin and traced his thumb across her lips. "Nervous?"

She nodded.

He smiled and the low hum of arousal flared up again. "Nervous is good. If you weren't nervous I'd be worried. Before we go any further, I want to know if you believe you can trust me."

She mulled the question for less than ten seconds. "I do."

"Mmm," His murmur of approval went straight to her clit. He leaned in and pressed his lips to her mouth in small sensual kisses. "You're right though. It's time to continue. It's time for us to get to know each other inside and out."

Before she could take a breath, he swooped forward and kissed her roughly. He didn't coax her mouth open, he simply growled and plunged forward, delving deep inside her. Every press and slide of his kiss felt perfect. Alternating teeth, tongue and lips, he devoured her in a kiss she felt in every nerve ending she possessed. Tori didn't know what to think--couldn't think. She felt edgy and overwhelmed. The clamps on her breasts pulled every time she wiggled and her pussy open and hanging over the edge of this damned chair made her ache from all the blood rushing to the area. If he kept her like this for long she'd beg or plead or scream.

In a show of need and desire, she bit at his lower lip and returned his possession of her mouth with everything she had. Tonight she wanted to be his. HIS.

Levi edged away, dropping kisses and bites as he traversed her chin, throat and neck. She flexed her hands and groaned in frustration when she couldn't move her arms to embrace him. He was too far away and still had his clothes on. Her imagination had been hard at work long enough over what lie underneath. He'd touched her just enough for her to get the impression he had not only an incredible body, but probably a penis that rivaled any man's. He'd felt huge.

With her mind going a mile a minute, she didn't notice how much he'd moved until Levi's evil hands grabbed the end of the clamps and tugged. She gasped. Fire raced through each nipple and spread through the rest of her. Oh my. In a short time he'd reminded her how sensitive her body could be when a man who knew what the hell he was doing touched her.

He nipped and sucked at the curve of each breast until she couldn't take it anymore. Her hands balled into tight fists, she pulled hard on her restraints and let loose a high-pitched wail that she'd have sworn came from someone else. Levi chuckled against her skin and kept working his way farther down her body. When his tongue hit her belly button she flinched against the insane level of pleasure. The ache between her legs became unbearable as moisture seeped from her sex.

"Levi, please!" she whined.

He didn't stop or acknowledge her. He simply went about driving her crazy without a care in the world. Tori tried to focus on her breathing. If she could relax she could control some of what she felt. She breathed in and out several times until finally her head fell against the back of the tall chair and she braced for what more he chose to give. Every cell felt swollen and needy. Her heartbeat pounded erratically in her ears, her nipples ached and her now engorged clit felt on fire.

"Please. Please. Oh God! Levi..."

He responded by sliding a finger between her slick and swollen folds. Her eyes rolled back in her head and she prepared to fight once again for control. "You're--you're making me crazy," she whimpered.

"I know. And I love it." One long finger sank inside her and Tori lost it. Her body shook and senseless words tumbled from her mouth that her brain couldn't even process. The first non self induced orgasm in years raced along her spine and built to epic proportions. She half thought her body would literally explode.

"What are you doing to me?"

"Whatever I want, baby, whatever I want." Another

finger pressed inside her and Tori screamed again. The pressure created by two fingers sliding inside her sent pleasure spiraling through her at the force of a category five tornado. She held her breath as he edged her closer and closer...

"Ask me to make you come," he demanded. His voice had changed. The easy going tone was long gone and had been replaced with a dark, delicious sound that felt every bit as incredible as his fingers fucking her nice and slow.

She didn't think she could form a word let alone a full sentence. Her mouth opened and nothing came out. His fingers had curled and swiped across the holy grail of sweet spots.

"Say it, Catori. Beg me to make you come before I change my mind and make you sit here like this while I eat dinner alone."

Her mind vaguely wrapped around his words. The part of her brain that wanted to defy him teased her as the word no sat on the tip of her tongue like a devious little devil daring her to be bad. It would be so easy. But his fingers were fucking magic and she wanted her release more. She panted for air. "Please, Levi. Oh. God. Please. Please. Dammit! Make me come."

To her delight, his thumb clamped down on her clit and the added pressure threw her into a tailspin. Her chest constricted as the air left her body in a sudden whoosh. Muscles tensed and released as layer after layer of sensation quaked through her. Fuuuuuuck.

"I feel your muscles trying to strangle my fingers. You're going to be really tight when I fuck you." His breath at her ear amplified everything. "Are you listening? This is me, Catori. Giving you what you need and taking what I need. Cry for me, baby because I need all of it. Every fucking word."

As if her body wasn't already out of control, his words bounced around her brain like jagged little impulses of pleasure determined to push her even farther. Then her thoughts exploded into tiny shards of nothingness. Her body turned to a mass of throbbing nerve endings all trying to devastate her. The moment his lips pressed to the small sensitive spot just behind her ear, she lost it all. Her mind, her body, her orgasm. Tori thrashed against the restraints as the spasms rocketed through her. Levi groaned into her neck as the scream tore from her mouth. His fingers never stopped, working her over until every last ounce she had to give had come exploding out. Her screams turned to cries that only stopped when her voice gave out.

When the gut-wrenching climax slowed, her body melted against Levi and the chair holding her up. Her mind started to war with the languishing pleasure. Feelings and emotions long buried came bubbling to the surface and she panicked. What the hell just happened? The bond she'd shared with Seth had been special. She wasn't supposed to have this kind of reaction to someone else. It felt like a betrayal to his memory. She tried to lift her head and say something but there was no energy to move yet. She had to get free. It was then she realized that tears were running down her face. A sob broke free. She couldn't contain her overflowing emotions.

"Catori, breathe."

Tori closed her eyes against him but nothing changed. Or maybe everything had changed.

THIRTEEN

Levi tried to pull it together. Tori sat in the chair bawling her eyes out and he'd done that to her. Fuck. He'd accomplished what he set out to prove with this little scene and then some. Yes, she needed to submit as badly as he needed to dominate. Whether she was ready to face that truth was another thing entirely. "Shhh, baby. It's going to be fine I promise. Just let me get you undone."

Holy hell, he couldn't breathe. Getting that deep inside Tori's head had been the most amazing experience of his life. His brain had nearly exploded when she came. If she hadn't started crying he'd probably have... *Stop. Don't go there.*

He unfastened her legs first as quickly as he could and rubbed the muscles along her inner thighs so it would hurt less when she tried to move them. She'd fought so hard against the restraints he knew tomorrow she'd be covered in bruises. He tried not to look at the marks on her skin, but he couldn't resist. How sick did it make him that the sight of the red streaks covering her arms and legs only made his dick harder?

As if he could get harder. Jesus H. It had been so damned good. He knew he'd never forget the sensation of her muscles clamped around his fingers and the sound of her screams rushing over his skin. They'd both seemed to love it right up to the point she started sobbing in his arms. How long had she been keeping these emotions bottled up? And why the hell was it so easy to accept them from her? So many times in the past he'd hit the road at the first sign of an emotional connection.

"C'mon, Tori. It's okay." He rubbed her arms and gently placed them around his neck. He dreaded the next part because he knew sometimes the clamps hurt a hell of a lot more coming off than going on and she didn't seem in the right frame of mind for any more pain. He undid the first one and dropped it to the floor. Her sob caught in her throat and he quickly caressed the tender nipple and breast until she started breathing again.

"I'm sorry, sweetheart. We've got one more." She nodded into the crook of his neck and he quickly undid the other before she could think it through. Her gasp traveled through him and straight to his cock before he could do anything about it. He'd always been more affected by the sounds a woman made in his arms than anything else. If he ever got inside her and she screamed like she'd done a few minutes ago he'd be done for.

He figured the pain had subsided by the way she'd begun struggling in his arms. Her jerky movements and sudden strength suggested panic or fear. Worried, he lifted her and enfolded her inside his arms. "Hang on, Tori. Let me get you some water and a blanket."

"Don't need--"

"You do but either way, I definitely need this. We need this." He swiped a bottle from the top of the bar and a blanket from the basket in the corner before he made his way to the loveseat positioned in front of the bay window that overlooked the downtown skyline. Once seated, he pulled her against his chest and wrapped the blanket around her shoulders. He uncapped the water bottle and tilted it to her lips. "Drink," he insisted. She took several small sips until she turned her head away. Levi stashed the bottle nearby and settled back with Tori in his arms. "Just rest. You have nothing to worry about. Needing to cry is nothing to be ashamed of or afraid of. But we're taking the time we both need to recover." After several long moments he noticed her muscles begin to relax. There were no more tears but no words either. Instead they sat and shared a blissful silence.

He stared out the window and watched all the lights in the distance twinkle. A week ago he'd been living in his tent and falling deeper into despair. Tonight he had an amazing woman fall apart in his arms. He wasn't convinced he deserved a woman like her, but that didn't mean he'd let her go. Instead he wondered what it would feel like to share all of his secrets with a woman he cared about. Would there ever be someone who could look at him without pity after she knew the truth?

The scent of sex and sugar drifted over him, distracting his thoughts. He couldn't help imagining being inside her now. The remembered sensation of the warm slick flesh of her pussy beckoned him. The many ways he wanted to fuck her ran through his mind like a particularly good porno flick. But most of all he wanted to lay her out on his bed, spread her legs and simply sink into her. The idea of making love to her all night long grabbed him by the throat and he didn't think it would ever let go. Not once in his life had he truly made love. He fucked. He satisfied and he dominated. Nothing remotely like love had ever entered the picture. He'd never allowed it to. Now he could think of nothing else. For the first time in his life, he felt more than simple lust. He wanted to savor her one inch at a time, mark her, make her his...

As if reading his mind, Tori shuddered over him.

"Just relax and let your mind go. I won't let anything

else happen to you I promise." The minute the words left his mouth his breath caught. The last time he'd made a promise like that everything had gone to shit. His stomach twisted at the rush of memories of his last operation in Afghanistan. He'd tried to keep the civilians out of the crossfire... Levi took a deep breath and tried to calm his racing mind. He'd be of no use to the sweet submissive in his arms if he got lost in the past. The past was the past and it was over. The familiar mantra repeated itself in his head several times before he started to feel a minimum of clarity.

Long minutes passed until he guessed they'd been sitting in silence for close to an hour. The fine tremors that had still been quaking through Tori had finally subsided. Her breathing evened out. She'd either fallen asleep or was on the verge of doing so.

"I'm sorry, Tori. I didn't mean to hurt you. I got carried away."

She sat up in his arms suddenly and turned on him fully awake, her eyes blazing. "What are you talking about? You didn't hurt me."

Taken aback by the fierce lioness crouched over him, he wasn't quite sure how to respond. She looked ready to pounce.

"The tears. I thought--"

"You thought wrong." She sat up, straddling his waist and he amazed himself when he managed not to roll his eyes to the back of his head at the sensation of her heat on top of him.

But if she wasn't crying because he'd hurt her... His mind went a mile a minute over the possibilities.

"It has been a really long time since I've done anything like that. I forgot how powerful it is to let someone else crawl inside my head and take over."

An intense pang of satisfaction shot threw him and quickly dissipated the second she moved again. With every twist and turn of her body he got glimpses of her pelvic positioned tattoo. He ached to lay her on a bed, slide between her legs and then trace the markings with his tongue.

As if to ensure she still had his full attention she moved again. This time she caressed him head to balls with nothing more than the thin cloth of his pants separating them. He ground his back teeth against the sizzling pleasure rushing through his veins. When she started to do it again he grabbed her hips and stilled her moves. "So now you plan to take the control back? Cause I'll tell you, sweetheart. That ain't happening."

"I was thinking more along the lines of simply getting you inside me."

That certainly got his attention. "Is that really what you want?" He trailed his hand from her shoulder to her neck before wrapping his fingers softly around her neck.

"Yes, Levi. It is."

Arousal hummed through his veins. Having her straddle his lap was an easy position to maneuver her through many things. "Open your mouth."

Her mouth dropped open and he slid a finger inside. "I want to play with you some more." He surged forward. "But more importantly I want to make love to you." He kissed her long, wet and deep, putting everything he wanted from her into his actions. "Can you think of any reason we shouldn't fuck?"

Her eyes widened and she shook her head.

He laughed. "I particularly like the deer in headlights look."

Tori punched his shoulder. "What do you expect? That's twice tonight you've said that."

Levi captured her wrists before she could swing at him again. "Said what?"

She dropped her head and stared at his chest. "What

you said."

"Look at me, young lady," he threaded the command with steel.

First her spine stiffened, then she lifted her head. The defiance shone loud and clear.

"Do you have a problem with the word fuck that I need to know about?" he asked.

"Not exactly. I've been known to say the word a time or two. I've just--" She started to turn a lovely shade of red. "I've never talked about fucking someone." Her head dropped into her hands and she shook her head back and forth. "I know it's stupid. It's the parent thing I guess, where I have to watch everything that comes out of my mouth lest it be repeated. Or maybe it's the fact I've only ever been with two men in my life." She shrugged. "I don't know."

Levi smiled. He laughed and smiled so much around Tori his face was beginning to ache. Damn she made him feel good. "Okay then." He bucked his hips one last time, letting her feel his erection against her gorgeous little clit. Her startled gasp made it difficult to let her go. With an inward groan he lifted her from his lap and placed her on her feet.

"How about that dinner?"

She scrunched up her face in obvious displeasure.

"No pouting or you'll end up at my feet while I eat the meal alone." He didn't really plan to follow through on that threat when there were far more clever ways to punish her, but damn if he didn't love the gamut of emotions that crossed her face. One of which he swore looked like anticipation.

"Should I even ask if I can have my clothes back on?"

He smirked. "What do you think?"

Tori rolled her eyes and then swept her arms in the direction of the dining table. "Fine. After you, your highness."

***

Levi glanced at Tori. She'd insisted on serving the food since she was technically on duty and he'd finally relented. In a matter of minutes she had everything artfully arranged and ready to eat. Her movements were graceful and well practiced. She'd obviously been doing this for quite some time. Albeit probably not with her tits bouncing as she did it.

She looked up. "May I sit?"

He didn't expect her to ask permission but he nodded to her anyway. Considering where they were, following a few more rules felt natural. However, his intention for the rest of the night was to make her more comfortable, not on her toes trying to make sure she did his bidding.

"Can I ask you something?" Her question interrupted his train of thought.

"Of course. In fact I was going to suggest we not worry about any more rules or protocols during dinner. It's not really my thing all that often. Hell, I'm a jeans and t-shirt kind of guy as you've seen."

"Which kind of leads into my question. Since I don't know you that well yet, I'm curious about what kind of work you do."

"Fair enough. Although it's kind of complicated." He linked his fingers with hers. "Might as well start from the beginning." He didn't know why he felt compelled to tell her everything, but the urge was strong. "When I was twenty-one I decided to drop out of college and join the Marines. Like a lot of kids that age I was more than ready to get out on my own and college wasn't my thing. I did the military thing for a long time and at one point I thought I'd be in it for the long haul."

"You changed your mind?"

"Afghanistan changed it for me. Let's just say things didn't go well for my unit and when I got sidelined with an injury the gig ended." He left a lot of the gory details out, but there wasn't much point in telling her that he'd been shot so many times it was a fucking miracle he'd lived. She'd know soon enough.

"You didn't come home after that?" Her question was innocent enough although the answer was far too complex.

"No. I didn't have any compelling reasons to return back then."

"But what about your parents? They must have been worried sick about you."

Levi braced himself for the jagged pain that came every time he thought of his mother. Her suicide had nearly decimated him and directly resulted in his leaving town. "Both my parents died while I was in college."

"Oh." The look of horror on her face distracted him from the turmoil churning in his gut. "I'm sorry, I didn't know."

"Of course you didn't and there's no need to apologize. It all happened a long time ago." She squeezed his hand this time and much of his hard outer shell began to break away. "So..." He wanted to move past the subject of either of his parents as quickly as possible. "While I recovered from my injuries I got bored and started messing around with some investments online. Over the years I saved most of my money so I had a fair amount to get started. Don't ask me how it happened, sheer luck I think, but a few of the companies I got involved with took off and my nest egg started to grow."

Her eyes got huge. "Wow. Seriously? I think that's the last thing I expected you to say."

His smile widened. "Let me guess. Unemployed biker? Maybe even part of a gang?"

She blushed fast and furious as her gaze shot down to her plate. "I didn't know what to think."

"Don't worry about it. If I'd seen me ride into town I would have imagined worse. I'd been camping in Utah for weeks and then on a whim decided to drive almost straight here with as few stops as possible and with little sleep."

"Why?" she asked.

Clever girl. Her curious and intelligent mind wanted more. "I haven't been back here for more than a decade. In the time between the Marines and now, I wandered a lot. Never settling too long in one place or another. I tried buying houses and settling down and it never took. Eventually I came to the conclusion there really was no place like home."

She nodded. "I can understand that. After Hannah's father walked out, I thought a lot about leaving. The idea of a fresh start far away held a lot of appeal. But ultimately I knew that Hannah and I would never be happy too far away from family. She loves spending time with my grandmother. That's where she is tonight. She'll be there for at least a few days before she'll be ready to come back home. Nana spoils her rotten."

"I think I've heard that's a duty of grandparents."

Levi watched her push the food around on her plate for the third time. "We're lucky to have her."

"What's wrong? Do you not like the pasta I ordered?"

Her head shot up. "What? No. The food is fine."

"Then what?" She looked so miserable. "Please be honest."

She placed her fork on the table and stared at him, her eyes large and sad. "I—" she hesitated. "I—this feels weird. Sitting here naked across the table with you fully dressed while we talk about family and stuff."

Levi puzzled through her answer and compared it to what he'd learned about her so far. When they'd been in scene she'd responded automatically with an eagerness he hadn't experienced in a long time. Afterwards she'd settled peacefully into his arms until he'd questioned her. But the minute he'd set her apart from him and started talking she'd fidgeted non stop and had barely touched her food. The scene had gone cold and her head was no longer in the right space. Their relationship was simply too new for this to work for her.

"How about we get dressed and blow this place? There's a great drive in burger place two blocks over where we can get the best damn burger on the planet and fried pickles to boot."

A wide smile crossed her face. "Really?"

He laughed. "Yes, really. Now come here."

Tori set down her fork and nearly leapt out of her chair. He grabbed her wrist and pulled her into his lap. He wanted to savor her nakedness for a few more minutes before she hid her glorious body from him. His hands roamed from her shoulders, down her arms and across her stomach before he cupped her breasts and gave them a light squeeze. "I think we should go somewhere away from all this where we can take our time and have the privacy we need to finish what we started earlier."

She turned toward him and pressed her lips to the side of his neck. "Your place is a bit of a mess. You want to come to mine?"

His dick throbbed insistently at the mere hint that he could have her naked again and in a bed in a matter of a short twenty-five minute drive. Instead he steeled his resolve in favor of his original plan. "I have a better idea. There's some property I'm thinking about investing in. A cabin not too far outside Asheville. I was going to invite you and

Hannah to accompany me this weekend, but since she's gone to play at grandmother's house, what do you say the grown ups go play in a cabin instead?"

She wriggled in his lap, rubbing that sexy ass across his aching dick.

"You wanted me and Hannah to go with you?"

"Of course I did. She's a great kid and a huge part of you that I'd like to get to know much better. Although my original plan included a tent and a fun campfire so we could all make smores."

"And now you want me to go alone with you to a cabin in the woods where you can seduce me?" Her teeth nibbled on his lower lip. Levi tightened his hands around her waist and ground her down on his cock.

"Your choice. Unless you're afraid the big bad wolf is going to eat you."

She cupped the sides of his face and stared up at him. "I'm counting on it."

FOURTEEN

Levi turned his motorcycle off the highway and Tori heaved a sigh of relief. She tightened her grip around his waist as he sped down the two lane road. As much as she'd enjoyed the last two hours plastered to his backside with the powerful vehicle vibrating underneath her, she was ready for this ride to be over. As promised he'd taken her to the drive-in and fed her the most amazing burger she'd had in years. Heck, she even ate some of his fried pickles, which had been a lot better than she'd expected.

At first the warm night air blowing underneath her helmet and the amazing view of the stars and moon above her had calmed the nerves plaguing her. Eventually however, she'd grown antsy to get to their destination. She'd had all this time to think about their earlier scene and it had done nothing except get her all hot and bothered all over again. Her breasts ached, her pussy throbbed mercilessly and her skin felt tight and uncomfortable. For the first time in years she looked forward to being completely naked in front of another person and it felt so damned good.

And scary as hell.

She needed to remember that this was only a three-night stand. Attachments weren't allowed. When the weekend was over they'd part ways and she'd go back to the not as exciting but solid life she'd built with Hannah. Neither of them were ready for anything more and she wasn't in any way shape or form ready for the consequences of someone like Levi learning the truth about her. Yet the memory of Levi practically looking inside her and pulling out her inner most needs with ease almost took her breath away.

Levi took another turn and the wide swath of his headlight gave her a good view of the heavily wooded area on either side of the road as he led her deeper into the woods surrounding the mountain. As much as she loved the small college town with easy access to a larger city she lived in, the solitude of this area also attracted her. It wasn't exactly a viable location for a good job or good schools for Hannah but it made the perfect weekend escape.

Before long, they slowed and turned onto a hard-packed gravel driveway leading to a gorgeous lake that reflected the moon shining down from above. They were still surrounded by trees and had yet to come across this mysterious log cabin he was taking her to. A few more minutes around the lake and Levi steered the bike to the left in another opening between two weeping willows.

His headlight hit the cabin and her mouth dropped open at the sight. For some reason she'd been expecting a small and possibly quaint isolated cabin and instead he'd taken her to the taj mahal of log cabins. In fact it looked big enough to be a lodge. He pulled up to the small cobblestone sidewalk that led to the front door and killed the engine. He then waited for her to get off before he did the same.

"This is what you call a cabin? This place looks insane."

He held up a key and shook it in front of her. "Want to go in and see the rest?"

"Definitely!" She followed him up the walk and

waited impatiently as he unlocked the large wooden door. They stepped over the threshold and she gasped. Deep leather couches flanked each door in front of two enormous stone fireplaces. All of the tables scattered around the room looked like they'd been hand carved directly from a tree. Straight ahead at the back of the room stood a large curved bar like a sentinel watching over the room.

"It is a lodge!"

"Converted lodge," he corrected. "Several years ago a well known real estate developer in the area took over the foreclosed property and began renovations. Apparently he's run out of financing and is looking for either a partner to help him finish the work or a buyer to take it off his hands.

She turned in a circle and took it all in. "So far it's incredible. You're thinking of buying it? I'm guessing the investments you mentioned working on have done very well."

He laughed. "Definitely well enough. Most of the investments I've tried my hand at have been real estate."

"Why? I always thought it was a volatile market."

"All the better for someone like me I guess." For a moment the light in his eyes dimmed and he got a far-off look that intrigued and concerned her. He had a past she wasn't all too sure she wanted the details of. What she'd learned already indicated nothing but hard times for him.

"You are a strange mystery, Levi Hawkins. And not what I expected."

He pulled her into his arms and lifted her chin. "Good. I prefer to keep you on your toes. What good am I if I can't surprise you?" It felt incredible to be in his arms again. He'd changed out of the dress pants and shirt he'd worn to Fire and Ice and the soft cotton of his button down denim shirt molded to the muscles underneath her fingers. Damn. She couldn't wait to see him naked. It was only fair.

"C'mon, let's go look for the master bedroom." He

grabbed her hand and led her down a long hallway that wound behind the lobby/living room area. Were they finally going to--fuck? See, she could at least think it.

They bypassed several closed doors and the inquisitor in her wanted to look inside each one. "How do you know where the master bedroom is? Have you been here before?"

"No. But the seller emailed me a series of detailed photos as well as an architectural drawing of the place."

Duh. Anyone in their right mind thinking about buying a place like this would have done his research ahead of time. "Are these all bedrooms" They'd passed at least ten doors already.

"Not exactly."

She stopped and dug in her heels. "What does that mean not exactly? What are they?"

He laughed. "Here, let me show you." He went back to the last door they'd passed, pulled a key card out of his pocket to unlock the door and went inside. She hurried behind him. For a second his ass encased in dark denim distracted her and she wondered what the hell was wrong with her. They could do a tour later. She wanted the bedroom or a table, or hell, the floor would suffice at this point. She'd been strung tight since their failed dinner and it was time to do something about it.

"See what I mean?"

His question jerked her from her thoughts and she blinked at him for a moment before she surveyed the room. Her mouth dropped open. There was a canopy bed in the middle of the far wall, a big, beautiful, hand-carved dark wood monstrosity covered in so many layers of silk she couldn't possibly count them all. But that was about the only resemblance to a bedroom. The walls were covered in rich dark purple fabrics from ceiling to floors with unique furniture strategically placed. A spanking bench in one corner, a sex swing in another and several tall cages grouped along the far wall.

"These are fantasy rooms. This one is the harem room. It's designed for large groups and accommodates just about anything they can think of."

Her tongue felt twisted in knots. Not in a million years had she expected he was taking her to a place like this.

"Don't be intimidated, Catori. This wasn't the room I had in mind for you." He held out his hand. "Shall we?"

Damn. The tone of his voice had changed again. The dark, husky sound went straight to her head and other places. There were a million questions whipping through her mind and she couldn't ask a single one. She placed her hand in his and followed him back out of the room. At the end of the hall, Levi opened another door and pulled her through. She suddenly found herself in an exotic sunroom with floor to ceiling windows that probably offered an amazing view that was too difficult to see in the dark. A swimming pool and hot tub combo took up the entire length of the room with patio seating set up in small groups around the perimeter.

She couldn't think about the expansive surroundings anymore with the warmth from Levi's hand zinging through her and the sound of his Dom voice still echoing inside her head. The slow burn in her body from the motorcycle ride was on the verge of turning into a volcanic fire. She barely noticed they'd gone through the pool room and walked up another flight of stairs until the last few steps. At the top the stairwell opened to an enormous loft-like master bedroom. It was like nothing she'd ever seen before. The bed filled one corner of the room and an open concept bathroom complete with spa tub filled the opposite end. To her surprise, there were no obvious pieces of BDSM equipment or furniture in the space. It simply appeared to be a luxurious spa-like bedroom with that really big plush canopy bed draped in silk and covered by a hundred pillows that looked like individual gems.

Levi grabbed her arm and twisted her around to face him. Her body reacted almost violently to the sensation of her front plastered to his tall frame. From her breasts to her thighs, heat fused them together enough to have moisture seeping from her sex. Her muscles clenched.

"It feels like I've been waiting forever for this moment," Levi said. "From the moment you bent over in front of me at the cafe to retrieve pie I've barely thought of anything else." His finger traced her lips, and she swore the heat between them rose another ten degrees. As if the tension rising between them had reached its threshold.

"I need to taste all of you." He bent forward and licked a path from the hollow of her neck to just below her ear. "But with you, I find myself losing the control I normally crave. I simply want to be inside you."

She moaned. Oh God, she expected her body to explode into flames any second if he kept teasing her like this.

"I'm going to have you my way and I'm going to be damned selfish about it," he warned.

"Yes." She so badly wanted him to need her even half as much as she needed him right now.

"I will take your submission and bend it to my will, Catori. *Mine.*"

A whimper escaped her as her body went limp in his arms. She was going to go out of her mind any second now. "Yours, Levi. Anyway you want it."

He growled and grabbed her ass, pulling her an inch higher so the head of his covered cock notched at the base of her clit. Her eyes rolled to the back of her head as the layers of sensation intensified. His other hand threaded through her hair and pulled her head back so she was forced to meet his gaze.

"Mine," he repeated a second before he crushed her mouth with his.

Her head swam with the implications of their situation. He'd just claimed her as his sub. Maybe more. Everything seemed as confusing as it did crystal clear. She strained to think of something other than giving him whatever he wanted for a few moments before giving in and kissing him back. She opened on a sigh as he unbuttoned her top and worked the fastening of her jeans. His hand plunged inside and directly into the wet heat awaiting him.

His fingers of one hand strummed her clit while the other pulled her hair tight enough to engage the pain sensation of a thousand little needles pressing into her skin. The pain warred with the pleasure until it all melded together and she exploded bright, hot and fast.

He wrenched free of her mouth. "Fucking A. You drenched my hand."

"I couldn't help myself," she panted.

He leaned forward and buried his face in her hair. "There's so much I want from you I'm not sure where to start. Other than the fact I will make you submit to me. It's now as important as the air I breathe." He pulled his hand free from her pants and worked them down and off her legs. Somewhere in his haste, she heard the telltale sign of her latest thong getting ripped again. When she stood naked in front of him he stepped back and studied her. His gaze traveled from her head down with a full stop when he got to her tattoo.

His hands reached for her hips and he rubbed his thumb across the claws. "Soon I want to hear about this, but not until after I've been so deep inside you nothing else matters."

Her stomach clenched and her legs quivered with every word. Every hot inch of her skin ached for more of him. Just him. That's all she focused on. That she was still able to stand of her own volition seemed like a miracle of epic proportions. He walked her back until her thighs met the back of the couch. He inserted his leg between hers and nudged her legs wider.

"Catori, just because you chose to put your submission away and focus on your daughter does not obliterate the well of need that will always simmer inside you." He bit at her neck and pinched her nipples to the point of sharp pain. "This is who you are. Embrace it."

She cried out. His words struck a chord deep inside her that refused to be ignored any longer. She wanted to be his at this moment and screw the three-night stand rule. What an idiotic idea that had been anyway. He wanted her submission and at this point she'd do anything for him.

"Anything, Levi. Please." He had to see how shaky she was. He made her weak and strong at the same time.

Levi shifted his body and pressed his hips forward. Her eyes rolled as the hard length of him pushed against her. Adrenaline flooded her brain as she realized that this is what she'd done to him. He wanted her. She shuddered with the thought. Maybe he ached right now as much as she did. With all caution gone she rolled her hips and met him move for move as they ground together.

Her actions were like setting a match to dry timber. They both combusted, Levi's eyes went so dark they no longer looked blue as his gaze bored into her, before he kissed her hard.

Without giving her a chance to catch her breath, he picked her up and threw her across the giant bed waiting for them. With one hand on her stomach he pinned her in place as he ripped at his clothes. The hunger etched across his face undid her as she fought to get him closer. All she could think about was him naked beside her, in her, over her...

He growled and she stilled. The animal look on his face mesmerized her. The Dom in him would take her in his own time with his own rules. She felt this clear to her core and it gave her a delicious thrill. She loved that whatever happened between them would be what he chose to happen and she'd freaking love it. He bent to his discarded pants and pulled something from the pocket. There wasn't a lot of light in the room except for the moon shining down through the skylight above her but it was enough to see he'd grabbed a condom.

"I'm on the pill," she blurted.

His head swiveled sharply and the vivid blue of his eyes returned. If someone could spontaneously combust, she was about to. "I'm clean," he offered. "And it has been quite some time since I've done this."

That did it. Her brain officially melted. The thought of such a virile man abstaining like she had amazed her. "How long?" she asked.

Levi tossed the small package to the floor and came over her. "I'm afraid you're in no position to ask the questions, young lady." His hot poker of a cock touched the inside of her thigh and she gasped. He was getting so close.

"You will come when I say so, is that understood?" His blue eyes held her immobile and mesmerized.

"Oh God. You're going to torture me aren't you?"

He didn't answer her question. Instead his fingers found their way down her body and worked her slippery folds with enough pressure to make her gasp again. Tension rose inside her and she feared she'd fail to wait for his permission to come.

"What if I can't wait?" she panted.

"You will." He assured her as he pushed two fingers deep inside her.

Tori arched her back and moaned, trying to stop the aching sensations that indicated this would be quick. More than ever she wanted to please him. But damn, the man had magic fingers that expertly worked every last nerve ending, including the--

Oh. My. God. His fingers rubbed across the tiny knot of nerves that shot a woman to no man's land the moment they were touched. She grabbed the silk comforter below her and balled it in her hands as she fought for some kind of control. His movements quickened and her vision dimmed at the onslaught of pleasure beyond her expectations. "You're going to make me come," she cried.

"Yes, I am and it's going to be heaven to watch. But not yet," he warned.

Tori clawed at the bed and then his shoulders. Her body climbed impossibly higher until she stopped breathing from the intensity. "Please. Oh God. Please, Levi. Don't make me fail."

"You'll never fail, my Catori," he whispered in her ear. In and out his wicked fingers moved and she still couldn't breathe. Spots danced in her vision and she was helplessly perched at the precipice exactly where he wanted her. Her mouth opened to scream and no sound emerged.

"There it is. Come now. Show me how much you love this."

Hard pulses inside her followed his words as she came screaming his name. He anchored her to the bed a moment more before he quickly withdrew and pressed the head of his cock between her folds. "Dammit, Catori. You are so fucking perfect."

He bent forward and bit down on her nipple until she cried out again and that finally broke him. He drove into her, stretching her more than she thought possible. Oh shit. So big.

He hooked on arm under her left knee and lifted it from the bed. This angle allowed him to get deeper still as he drove into her repeatedly. His breathing grew as ragged as hers with each new thrust. Sweat beaded on their skin and the scent of musk and sex assaulted her senses. Tori couldn't move or speak. She was helpless to do anything other than take whatever he wanted to give. The layers of pain that had hardened her heart to a man like Levi began to crumble. He pumped harder while never taking that blazing blue gaze from her face that said he saw her. In submission she could not lie.

"So fucking perfect," he repeated.

"Yes," she cried.

"Come again," he said with the muscles of his neck obviously straining.

The next stroke lit the fire and she convulsed with the first layer of release. It came in waves with her muscles sucking and pulling him harder on each movement. She grabbed his shoulders and held him tight when the screams overtook her.

He kept going.

Both of them bucked and fought as sanity deserted them in the face of power fueled pleasure. She alternately screamed and sobbed as her body gave in and clutched him wildly. In a mad frenzy they came together this time with his fevered cry ringing in her ears as he emptied inside her.

Levi collapsed and rolled, keeping her leg high and wrapped around his hips. The perfect position that allowed him to stay inside her. Their breathing eventually slowed, but Tori's heart still beat like a frightened jackrabbit. Nothing had ever been quite like that and now she truly understood what it meant to be fucked. Emotions were rioting like Mexican jumping beans inside her as she attempted to regain her equilibrium and failed.

They laid there for quite a while without either of them moving, sated for now. Being alone with him and comfortable in silence felt like heaven. Tori stroked the arm he'd draped across her stomach and reveled in her surreal surroundings. This wasn't at all what she'd expected when she'd went to work tonight--er--technically yesterday now. She had no idea what time it was, but it wouldn't surprise her at all if the sun came up soon. A slight whimper escaped her at the thought of morning bringing an end to this incredible night. She wasn't ready. Josie'd been right, Levi was certainly not the kind of man you got out of your system with a one-night stand.

Levi's hand slid across her stomach and to her breast. Lightning streaked through her chest and a small moan filled the room. He shifted inside her and she gasped to discover he'd started to harden.

"Again?" she asked.

"Never going to get enough," he bent down and sucked a nipple into his mouth. She was already hard, too.

FIFTEEN

Somewhere far away, Levi heard a phone ring. He tried to roll away from the sound, pulling Tori tighter against him in the comfort of the bed. Why did he ever decide to get one of those damn things anyway? It meant people would call him and he'd be expected to talk to them. Another insistent ring sounded and Levi grabbed a pillow to cover his head.

On the third ring Tori stirred. "What is that?" she groaned.

"It's just my phone. Don't worry about it. Whoever it is calling at this ungodly hour can leave a message or call back."

"You realize it's probably at least noon by now, right? I don't think that's considered ungodly," she drawled.

Tori stiffened next to him as the damn device rang again. "Shit." She threw back the covers and scrambled from the bed. "That's *my* phone and I've gotta get it. Hannah…" She dove across the room, in an amazing display of grace that seemed to deny how sore she had to be, and dug through the clothes they'd left piled near the bedroom door. Watching her in a free moment rushing for her phone without a guard that needed to be knocked down came at the perfect time. His cock already stood at attention and saw an opportunity to continue its wild ways from the night before *and* earlier this morning.

"Hi Nana, how's Hannah?" Levi heard the frantic voice all the way across the room and his body went on immediate alert even before Tori's body went board stiff.

"Slow down I can't understand you. What did Hannah do?"

The vague uneasiness crawling over him turned into full alarm when he watched the blood drain from Tori's face and the phone drop out of her hand.

"What's wrong?" Out of bed and by her side in a flash he scooped up the phone and pressed it to his ear. Tears sprung from Tori as she dug through the clothes and began trying to dress herself.

"Hannah's gone. Bill took her. Her father." Tori's words were hardly intelligible through the sobs racking her body. "Oh my God. Oh my God. Why? What does he want? We haven't heard a peep from him in ages."

All very good questions he wanted answers to as well. He thrust the phone in Tori's face. "Talk to your grandmother and repeat everything I say." He put an extra level of command in his voice he knew she'd automatically obey. They didn't have time for her breakdown right now.

She blinked several times, tears still streaming down her face. Her eyes were already red rimmed and a huge section of her hair hung across her face that she didn't even bother to move.

Fortunately she'd heard what he'd said and the order got through. "Nana, calm down."

"Ask her how long ago Hannah was taken." She repeated the question.

"Less than ten minutes ago." Her voice shook.

"Good. What was he driving?"

She listened to her grandmother before she spoke.

"Some kind of black car. She didn't get a good look at it."

"Two doors or four?" All these little details could make a difference if push came to shove.

"Four."

"Okay. Tell her to stay calm. We're on our way."

"What about the police? We need to call them. Get their help."

"Not yet. Let me make a call first. Hang up."

She spoke a few more seconds to the woman at the other end and then disconnected the call. Levi finished dressing in a matter of seconds. All the information from Tori's grandmother was flying through his brain, mentally being catalogued for when he'd need the information quickly.

"Give me the phone." Tori tossed it to him.

"Who are you going to call? We don't have time for that. We need to be on the road right now." The rising hysteria showed in the crack of her voice. "I can't believe this is happening. It's been more than a year since we've spoken and not once in all this time has he shown an ounce of interest in Hannah. Oh my God. He hates me. What is he going to do? Why now? Shit. I never should have left her."

"Catori." His voiced boomed through the room. She lifted her head and met his gaze. "Stay calm. We're heading out as soon as I make this call. Grab your gear and meet me in front of the cabin." He punched in the one phone number he'd ever memorized and put the phone to his ear. He ignored the insistent buzz in his head. There was no time for a lick of emotion in this situation or a trip down memory fucking lane. Hannah needed him.

"Levi, is that you? What's wrong? Why are you calling me from Tori's phone?" Mason barked.

Levi ground his teeth at the condescending tone. "Of course it's me. You know I'd never give this phone number to anyone unless I was dying."

"Glad to hear you're not dead then. Is anyone else?"

"Tori's daughter has been kidnapped by her ex. We just got the call from her grandmother where Hannah was staying for the night."

"Shit. Are you kidding me? Levi, I told you to stay away from her. Can't anyone follow directions anymore? I don't make these rules on a whim you know?"

"I don't know what the hell you're talking about but you can bitch at me later. Tori and I are two hours away and we need your help. I need you to find out everything you can on," he turned to Tori, "What's his last name?"

"Don't bother," Mason interjected. "I already know his name and every detail we could need down to what fucking cereal he eats for breakfast."

Levi's blood ran cold at that little nugget of intel. He didn't understand it but he knew Mason well enough to know if he'd had Bill investigated there was a very good reason. Which gave him all the more reason for Mason to handle the situation until he and Tori got back. The man's ultimate talent was his devious nature and ability to stay calm under any circumstance.

"I hope you're ready for the shit to hit the proverbial fan," Mason said.

Levi rolled his eyes and ignored Mason's drama. "I'll be there in two hours. See what you can do about this mess. If I have to hunt this asshole down no one is going to like the outcome."

The line clicked dead. Fucking, Mason. Bastard made sure everyone knew who was in charge.

"What was that all about? Who were you talking to?"

Levi turned around and came face to face with Tori's tear streaked cheeks. The emotional devastation and fear he recognized grabbed his gut and kicked him in the balls. Suddenly his vision wavered and time disappeared.

Nina stood in front of him, barely eighteen and covered in so much fucking blood. Her eyes were wild and unfocused as she stared past him to Tucker. At her feet, Levi's father lay motionless, more blood pooling around him.

What are they doing here? Nina's voice was hoarse, vacant. He took a closer look and saw red, angry welts on her arms and one of her eyes was swelling shut as if she'd recently been hit. What the hell had happened here tonight?

Levi rushed forward to check for a pulse and as expected he found none. His father's lifeless body was now as cold as his heart. *It's too late.*

Tucker? Nina's voice turned hysterical.

Jesus, Nina. What the hell happened? How did this happen?

Instead of answering she grabbed Levi's arm and pulled him off balance. *You shouldn't be here.* She shrieked.

Yes they should. These men are our brothers. Tucker broke the news to his sister as effectively as knocking her upside the head. *Apparently the bastard has been knocking up women left and right. Some religious mumbo jumbo.*

Nina's shoulders shook and she slid to her knees. Mindless of the blood, she dropped her head in her hands and wept. All three men glanced at each other, hoping someone would have a clue what to do right now.

Mason grabbed Levi's arm. *Do you smell that?*

What? He sniffed at the air and the scent of something burning hit him. *Fire!*

Smoke poured into the room, followed by a racing line of flames.

Tucker, get her out of here. Mason took charge and began issuing orders. Nina's sobs turned to a loud wail. Before anyone could protest, Mason stepped forward and pulled the knife from their father's chest. Levi stood and stared in shock as Tucker grabbed his sister and lifted her over his shoulders and rushed from the house.

Don't get dumb on us now, Levi. Get the hell out before the whole house goes up in smoke.

He took one last look at his dead father before he turned and followed his newly discovered brothers out of the burning building. At the front door, flames were already licking at the walls and setting the curtains on fire. The whole damn situation raged out of control.

Wait. Stop. STOP! Nina pounded on Tucker's back until he plopped her on her ass on the front lawn. She immediately scrambled to her feet and attempted a run for the house. Levi grabbed her around the waist and pulled her back to safety.

No. No. NO. Let me go. We can't leave her.

Her? All three men spoke in unison.

Your mother. Tucker your mother is still in there.

"Levi. Earth to Levi. Levi, snap out of it." Tori's shouts and the fact she was shaking him as hard as she could yanked him back to the here and now.

"What? Oh sorry," he responded.

"Where the hell did you go? I couldn't make much sense of what you were saying."

"Sorry, I was thinking and got carried away." Then her words sunk in. "What did I say?"

Tori narrowed her eyes and pursed her lips. "Don't try to distract me now. Who did you call?"

"Mason. If anyone can figure out what's going on while we travel, it will be him."

"And what you said a second ago. He and Tucker are your brothers? Literally? Tucker as in Nina's brother and Mason the billionaire from Purgatory?"

Oh shit.

***

After the longest two hours of her life, Tori finally rushed into her grandmother's house. She'd placed several calls to Bill's cell phone and so far he'd not responded to any of them. Frantic, she ran to the family room hoping upon hope that it had all been a mistake and she'd walk in on her and Nana playing a game or knitting some new project.

What she walked into was far different than anything she could have expected. Her grandmother stood at the back door staring outside and Tucker and Mason sitting on the couch looking far too large for the tiny living room. Despite Levi's shocking revelation that these men were his brothers, they were still basically strangers to her and it didn't feel right to involve them in such personal business. "Why are you here?" she demanded.

A hand touched her shoulder and an immediate shot of comfort zipped through her. "They're here because they want to help. Because I asked them to."

"What's happening with Hannah? Has anyone heard from Bill?"

Before either man could speak, her grandmother turned and Tori got the first look at her devastation. She was not a young woman to begin with, but overnight she looked as if she'd aged ten years. Instead of the vibrant, loving woman she'd leaned on her whole life, she now looked fragile and ready to break at any moment.

"I'm so sorry, Catori. I never would have opened the door if I'd thought anything like this could happen." Tori's heart broke all over again at the anguish in her grandmother's voice, it was too painful. She closed her eyes and wished for an escape. Or that she'd wake up from this particular nightmare.

"Nana it's not your fault. Not once has Bill ever turned his anger or petty bullshit on my child. Never in a million years would I dream he'd want to hurt her."

"What? Are you telling me this bastard has hurt you in the past?" Levi's face turned dark red and the violence in his own eyes shocked her.

"Calm down, Levi," Mason muttered. "No one is going off half cocked until we get a handle on this."

Tori turned on Mason. "Levi has been anything but half cocked. If not for him, I would have either broken down or gone on a murderous rampage by now. I don't know how well you two know your brother, but I'm getting the impression not well."

Mason's eyebrow cocked in her direction a moment before his gaze cast to Levi behind her. Tucker on the other hand clamped his mouth shut and she got the impression he was trying not to smile. Not that any of them had a damn thing to smile about right now.

A cough sounded from the direction of the kitchen and a sliver of hope stabbed through Tori. She turned to investigate and was shocked to find her boss filling the doorway, a strange look on his face. The false bravado she'd embraced to get this far crumbled. Gabe, Tucker, Mason and Levi all in the same room was too much. The overload of testosterone was enough to strangle her. Gabe must have sensed her impending breakdown as he crossed the room in three strides and enfolded her in his arms.

She breathed in his cologne and let the familiarity of a man she not only knew as well as anyone could but also trusted implicitly provide some much needed comfort.

"Brothers, huh?" Gabe questioned. "Guess that explains a lot. Although it also raises a series of new questions."

"Fuck. Why don't we just take out a fucking ad in a fucking newspaper and tell the whole damned world." Mason pushed his hand through his hair and stood to his full height of well over six feet. Again, she was reminded that these overpowering men were in her grandmother's house. Before she could make a move to speak, she was pulled from Gabe's embrace and up against Levi's hip. The possessive move made her weak in the knees. He'd all but thumped his chest and proclaimed her as his in front of all these people who were now his family.

"This isn't about us," Tucker reminded them all. "It's Hannah we should be concerned with. We'll figure out how to deal with the rest later."

"I look forward to hearing all about it." Gabe looked unsettled to say the least. It made her curious about how he fit into all of this.

"Has anyone heard from this asshole?" They all turned to her grandmother when Levi asked the question.

"No. Like I was telling these gentlemen before you got here. He showed up and had Hannah out the door in a matter of minutes before I could do anything. Hannah was so happy to see him I was afraid to scare her."

Tori went to her grandmother and hugged her. Her pillar of strength all these years now needed her comfort. "It's okay, Nana. This is not your fault. You did the right thing. The last thing I want is for Hannah to be scared right now. Hopefully you not freaking out kept Bill calm and my daughter safer." She kissed the woman on her cheek. "Thank you for loving my daughter as much as I do."

"Oh, Catori. Your Hannah is my greatest pleasure. The rest of the family is missing out over their stupid pigheadedness."

She offered her grandmother a smile before she turned back to the four overgrown men still crowding the space.

"What about the police? As much as I don't think he'd harm Hannah, I'm still worried. Isn't time crucial in these types of cases? Bill definitely has the resources to disappear quickly if that's what he wants."

Mason broke rank and stepped toward her. "We've

got two things hopefully on our side. One. I've dealt with Bill Bennett in the past and I know how he does things. Second, whether or not the police can help depends on what your child custody agreement says. Do you have a copy I can provide my lawyer? He's standing by outside the police station awaiting my word."

Tori dropped her head and fought the tears that refused to leave. "There isn't one," she whispered, shame whipping through her.

"What?" All four men echoed in unison.

"I know what you're thinking, but there really was no reason to get one. He swore he wanted nothing to do with me or Hannah. So please don't lecture me."

Mason pulled out his phone and tapped out a text. "Unfortunately, North Carolina law is pretty explicit in these instances and unless we can prove some sort of danger that social services can get involved in, the police won't be able to do much. Without a custody agreement he has as much right to her as you do and only a court can decide otherwise."

Tori felt the blood drain from her head. She swayed and Levi lunged for her, catching her before she dropped to the ground. "That can't be. He hasn't cared for her at all. Never more than a few hours at a time anyway. Not once has he spent one night alone with her." Tears were falling onto her cheeks and she didn't care. Her baby. She couldn't live without her baby.

"Shhh, Catori." Levi brushed the tears from her face as quickly as they fell. "You are mine now and that makes Hannah matter to me even more. That bastard won't get away with this. I promise."

"Levi, don't," Tucker warned.

"Shut up. You don't understand." Tori watched Levi lash out at his brother in sort of a surreal slow motion.

"The hell I don't. You think I haven't broken our

pact repeatedly with, Maggie? I know exactly how you're feeling right now. But some promises are too dangerous and there are things you don't know about all this."

Tori tuned them out. All she could focus on was the image of her beautiful daughter crying for her momma. Tori sobbed harder. Everything she'd tried to hold in for the last couple of hours poured out of her. Levi tried to comfort her and she heard nothing. Memories of her past and present crowded every inch of available space in her head. Seth's death had started a chain reaction that had led her to Bill. Which eventually had turned into the colossal mistake she couldn't escape from. And yet, never in a million years would she have expected something like this.

But if Bill hurt one hair on her head or made her shed a single tear...

He would pay for it with one body part at a time. Mason was right about one thing. Without cops, there would be no one to get in her way. Violence ran strong in her blood and she was prepared to unleash hell on earth to get her child back.

SIXTEEN

"We need to talk. Privately." Mason tipped his head in Tori's direction and Levi got the message loud and clear. His brother had something to say he didn't want her to hear.

He turned Tori in his arms and tilted her head until their gazes met. He wiped away the remaining wetness from her cheeks and pressed a slow kiss to her lips. "Can you stay here with your grandmother for a few minutes while Mason, Tucker and I step outside to talk?"

"Yes. I've got my big girl panties on now. I'll be fine."

Her sarcasm did nothing to loosen the knot continuing to twist in his gut. Her sobs had disappeared and a new too calm resolve seemed to come over her. He wanted her to talk to him, share what was going on in that brain of hers, but he needed to find out what Mason knew about this Bill Bennett before he could define the parameters of the rest of this mission.

He kissed the top of her head and glanced over at Tori's grandmother. Deep worry lines were etched across her olive skin, but she appeared calm and able to help Tori if she needed anything. "I'll be right outside. If you need anything or if Tori does, please come and get me." The woman nodded and Levi reluctantly released his hold on the woman in his arms.

"Let's go." He led the way out the front door and headed to Mason's car. It had to be Mason's. Dark, sleek and very expensive. He had no qualms at all about spending their father's blood money. For Levi, the thought revolted him. Every time he'd even considered it he saw his mother's body sprawled on the floor with half her head blown on the wall. A shudder worked over him and he fought to suppress the memory. One memory would lead to another and the next thing he knew another anxiety attack would take over and they'd all be in deep shit.

He steered them all far enough away from the house so he was certain no one would overhear before he spun on Mason and Tucker. "Okay. We're alone. What have you got?"

"You're not going to like it." Tucker warned.

"Why are you here anyway? What happened to the laying low until things calmed down?"

"Really? You want to ask me that now? What about you? How many years has it been since I've heard from you in any other way than a report from Mason?"

Tucker's anger wasn't exactly misplaced. He'd resented the hell out of Mason and Tucker who both still had their mothers and their lives here and over the years that resentment had done nothing but grow.

"Fighting isn't going to help the situation. Might as well put the cards on the table and then you can figure out how to blow them up later." Tucker and Levi both nodded and gave Mason their full attention.

"I didn't have to lift a finger to research Hannah's father because I already know everything about him and when I say everything, I truly mean everything."

"Okaaay. So what's the big deal? You know the guy. That's good right? You know where we can find him? So what the hell are we doing standing around here like a god damned coffee klatch. We've got to get that child back in her mother's arms today."

Mason held his hand up to Levi. "Hold on there, Tonto. It isn't as easy or uncomplicated as you might think." Mason pulled out his keys and depressed a button on the key fob for his car. The lights blinked twice and the alarm chirped. "I'm going to have to show you."

His brother retrieved a file from the front seat. "Hannah's father is Bill Bennett. Thirty years old from Raleigh, graduated from North Carolina State about eight years ago with a degree in philosophical studies and then entered seminary school. Right after college he married his high school sweetheart and they had two kids." Mason paused before he continued and Levi got a sick feeling that it was what came next that would change everything.

"He started an internship at The Church of God & Light."

"Wait. What? I thought they got shut down years ago after you cut off all their funding."

"They did. Unfortunately our illustrious father had some very serious followers who couldn't let it go so they moved away from Davidson and started all over again near Raleigh. It wasn't until years later I even heard about it." He dug through some papers until he found what he was looking for. "I try to keep up with all of our blood relatives who the charity supports, but for some reason this nugget slipped by me until Tori's background check brought it to my attention."

Oh God no.

"If you tell me that Catori is somehow related to us..."

"Relax. I'm not. At least not by blood. Tori however, is the mother of your, or really *our* niece, i.e. Bill Bennett is one of our dickhead father's many children.

We've been supporting him in one way or another all his life. And let me tell you, his life is uglier than you can imagine. Over the years I've slowly cut back on his funding. I couldn't stomach him using it to fund that bullshit church."

Levi sagged against Mason's car, trying to take it all in. This went beyond dumb luck and straight into what the fuck territory.

"Has the church modernized? Or are we looking at a group of fundamentalists with radical ideas again?" Tucker asked.

"You have no idea how much I hate even referring to them as a church. They don't deserve such a respectable title. And yes, to answer your question, they have maintained their narrow vision and self righteous judgmental attitudes." Mason closed the folder. "This situation is beyond impossible."

Levi grabbed the information from Mason and rifled through the many papers himself that included a copy of Hannah's birth certificate listing Bill Bennett as the father. None of this made sense. "There's no doubt I've stepped into a mess. But what does this have to do with Hannah and Tori though?"

"I'm not entirely sure but I have my suspicions about this Bill Bennett. Over the years there have been subtle inquiries as to where his *scholarship* money came from. And he's not the only one. My guess is that these kids are growing up and some of them are either more curious for their own good or down right suspicious. Despite the great lengths we've gone to, nothing is infallible."

"That's just fucking great." Tucker shoved his hands into his hair and snarled.

"Of course that doesn't mean I can't gather my own information. We know how that church operates and I have a fine investigative team that is paid handsomely for good information."

"None of this is helping me get Hannah back in her mother's arms right now." Levi grappled with the need for certain action versus all this damned speculation. "Why the hell aren't we chasing this fucker down?"

"Let me put this in terms I think you'll understand. We aren't going anywhere until I have every shred of intel available to me. The last thing we need is anyone getting hurt or another cluster fuck."

"Fuck you, Mason. You go ahead and sit on your Gucci covered ass while I get the job done. I don't give a shit." He had already memorized the pertinent details in the folder such as address and contact information. That's all he needed to gather his own damned intel.

"You little ungrateful shit." Mason grabbed Levi by the neck, his fingers pressing into pressure points that took him by shock. By sheer will he managed to stay on his feet and fight the stranglehold of his brother.

"Dammit, Mason. Let him go. You two are acting like two teenage boys in a pissing match. We have bigger problems than fighting each other." Tucker stepped between them. "Let. Him. Go," he ordered.

A phone rang, breaking their focus. Mason reached into his pocket and pulled out a smart phone. "Unknown number."

"Answer it," Levi and Tucker said in unison.

"It could be important." Levi's gut told him the call wasn't a coincidence.

Mason depressed the call button and released his grip on Levi's neck. "Who is this?" he growled into the phone. He must have gotten an answer and not liked it. The anger he'd expressed towards Levi was nothing compared to the dark look that took over his features at whatever the caller said.

"Where is the girl?" he asked.

Fuck.

Levi dove for the phone and Mason evaded him. Tucker again stepped between them. "Don't. This is what he does best, you dumbass. You wanted our help so let us help. If anyone can negotiate Hannah's return safely, it's him."

Levi nodded at Tucker and pressed his fingers against his closed eyes. All of the information Mason had shared had his brain on overload. He didn't want to think about the whys and the what ifs this new situation implied. Now he was pretty sure the kidnapping asshole was on the phone with his brother and the murderous rage building in his head was enough to have his back teeth grinding and his fists clenching.

Standing by in the midst of chaos had never been his strong suit. Lead or get the hell out of the way. Those were the words he lived by and ultimately became part of the reason he'd left the military. The time had come to get the hell out of the way.

"Let's talk. But first you have to return the girl. Clearly you've got the upper hand with or without her so there's no need to use her as a pawn."

Levi tensed. Mason talked to the guy like it was no big deal. As if the beautiful child with the big brown eyes and wild curly hair and easy smile was no big deal. He glanced at the house and imagined Tori's panic if she knew Mason was on the phone with Hannah's father negotiating for her return in the same way he did any other business deal.

"No. You either return the girl first or we're done talking."

Silence stretched out as Mason listened. Tucker and Levi exchanged glances and he recognized the same tension keeping him coiled tight.

"Fine. One hour. I know where it is." Mason disconnected and shoved the phone in his pocket.

"Get in. The Bennett asshole is willing to return the girl but we can't be a minute late or he's gone and it's going to take us an hour to get there."

"What? Is Hannah okay?" Levi looked back at the house once more. "I've got to update Tori."

"There's no time. Yes she's fine. But we have an hour to come up with a plan that not only gets Hannah back to her mother, but protects us from the scandal this shithead is about to unleash."

"Scandal?" This time Tucker cut in. "We can't afford anymore scandal right now."

"Tell me something I don't know. And the little bastard knows it. He's pieced together enough information to make him dangerous."

With the barest of hesitation, they all three climbed into the car. "What does he want?"

Mason rolled his eyes. "What the hell do you think? He wants what every asshole on this planet wants. Money."

***

Tori stared at the big grandfather clock in her grandmother's living room and waited. Tick tock. Tick tock. Every second that damn thing made some kind of noise and she now sat strung out like a live wire with nowhere to direct the adrenaline. She'd been waiting for hours. An hour after the men had disappeared outside to supposedly talk, she'd given up waiting and gone outside to figure out what they'd planned. This sitting around and doing nothing had her on edge and she wanted some action.

Instead she'd found an empty yard and Mason's car gone. All three of them had slipped away without so much as a single word. Her mind reeled with the myriad of implications their disappearance could mean. Did they know something she didn't? Had they gone hunting for Bill? Her head pounded as the unanswered questions nearly vomited from her brain. She squeezed her eyes shut and tried to focus on something that could stop the out of control sensations.

She thought about Levi and the scene earlier in the day just before they left cabin. He'd gone somewhere. Had slipped into some old memory that made her blood run cold. Even without all the details, the way Levi's face had transformed with a look of horror and fear gave her more insight than she knew what to do with. Not to mention the revelation he had two brothers. Tucker Lewis and Mason Sinclair. If there were three more unlikely men to be related she couldn't imagine. She knew a little about Tucker through Nina, his sister and a woman she now called friend. He was some sort of rich artist and until recently a bit of a recluse.

He'd recently reconnected with a woman he fell for in high school and they'd gone up north for her to teach some class about sex. It had all sounded a little too surreal to her. She stood and paced behind the couch. She'd forced her grandmother to lie down for a while and promised she'd let her know the second she heard something. Tori on the other hand, could barely sit still. Every few minutes she checked her phone for any missed calls. She'd left countless messages for Bill who'd yet to return a single one and Levi's phone still sat on the counter where he'd left it earlier.

She pictured the three men off attempting some sort of rescue like the three musketeers and had to cover her mouth to keep from laughing out loud. Levi she could see getting into a physical altercation with Bill, Tucker maybe... But Mason? She knew the least of all about him. Until now she'd never seen him anywhere but at Purgatory and Fire and Ice. More so at the restaurant. He always appeared in an expensive business suit and if he knew how to smile, she'd never seen it.

He glared a lot. And always dined alone. Except for Gabe. She rounded the couch and headed to the dining room where her boss had set up shop. He'd been on the phone since the minute she reported the others were gone. She'd tried grilling him for more information and he'd only told her that he'd inform her as soon as he had something concrete. Was this what dealing with Doms all the time would be like? Seth had been a gentle Dom outside the bedroom. Sure he'd set some small guidelines for her, but they'd spent more time apart than together so she'd never experienced a true long term relationship like that.

And then there was Bill... *Nope not going there right now.*

She found Gabe, phone in hand and a dark expression across his face. "I don't want to hear excuses, I just want it done." He motioned for her to take a seat and Tori took the one he indicated like the good little submissive she was supposed to be.

A second later, Gabe clicked off the phone without so much as a goodbye to whomever he'd been talking to. "You need to relax, I can hear your constant pacing all through the house. I'm sure your grandmother can too."

Tori frowned. "Really? You expect me to sit here quiet as a church mouse while I wait for some miracle to return my child?"

Gabe sighed. "No, Tori. I'm just thinking all this anxiety is a waste of time. Mason has made contact with that asshole ex of yours and he's currently in negotiations with him. And reports are that Hannah is perfectly fine."

"What?" She jumped from the chair. "You knew all this and you're just now telling me? Where are they? What does Bill want?" She slapped her hands on the table and blew out a hard breath. "What the hell is going on?"

"I just told you everything I know and I only heard from Tucker about three minutes ago. I was headed in to tell you when I got off the phone."

Fuck. All she wanted to do was scream and stomp and throw things. Not once in Hannah's young life had she not known exactly where she was and who she was with at all times. The relief she should feel right now never materialized. "I want my child, Gabe."

He rose and came around the table. "I know you do, sweetheart, and I can't even imagine the anguish you must feel right now. But I promise you, one way or another Hannah will be coming home to you very soon. Mason will make sure of that."

"How can you be so certain? I don't know this Mason at all. Until today I'd never so much as spoken to him. Why would he care about my daughter?"

"Because Mason cares about all of his employees."

Tori stared at Gabe, dumbfounded. What was he saying? "Mason is the owner of Purgatory?" Tori had just assumed that Gabe owned the club. He was the only one who'd ever appeared to run the place.

"He is one of the owners. I guess after today we could call it a family business." The frown on his face indicated his own displeasure at some of today's revelations.

Tori dropped into one of the empty chairs and tried to organize everything that had happened. "You're saying that all three of them own it? But they're never there. I thought Levi hadn't lived here since he was a kid."

"For the most part they are silent partners. Mason takes a small active role but as far as everyone knows, I'm the manager and presumed owner and we all like it that way."

Curious. "How well do you know them?"

Gabe looked thoughtful as he considered his answer. "We all went to college together. I came on board shortly after they opened the club. Then Tucker's father died and Levi's mother killed herself. Pretty much after that nothing was the same. Levi left town and joined the military, Tucker withdrew from life and Mason became the CEO of the conglomerate Tucker inherited in his stead.

Tori's head ached with all the information overload. "Levi's mother killed herself?" The idea made her heart hurt.

Gabe grabbed Tori's hand and drew her gaze to his. "I probably shouldn't be telling you all of this, but you need to know what kind of men you're dealing with. They all may be stubborn as the day is long, but they've all been through hell and their loyalty knows no bounds. If you and Levi are together, then that makes you family and they'll do anything for family. Plain and simple."

Tori pulled free and crossed the room. Her arms wrapped around her waist as she huddled against the window overlooking the small front yard. "Levi and I aren't together like that. I had a moment of weakness and thought I could do a temporary fling. That's ended now. All that matters is I get Hannah back and we try to get back to normal."

"Is that what you want, Tori? Normal? Even you must know better than that."

She couldn't think beyond her child. Even a temporary loss of Hannah had taught Tori a very important lesson. Her personal needs paled in comparison to the responsibilities of motherhood. She'd already lost one person she loved more than life, no way could she go through that again.

"Tori?" Gabe's voice broke through her thoughts. He'd moved closer and softened his tone. He touched her shoulders. "Don't let this setback shut you off from what you need. Sometimes ignoring the very base of who you are can end up being self destructive even when that isn't what you intended."

Tori didn't turn or respond. She couldn't. The tears burning her eyes wouldn't allow it. First Seth, then the betrayal of Bill to a life she could never embrace, to the potential loss of her child. She covered her face and let the tears she couldn't stop if she wanted to flow freely.

"Take your hands off of her."

A sudden chill swept over her while heat infused certain parts of her body. Instinctively Tori turned at the sound of Levi's voice. To her shock, he stood in the doorway with a sleeping Hannah in his arms.

Tori rushed forward. "Oh my God, is she all right?"

"She's fine. Better than fine actually. She was non stop chatter until she fell asleep in Mason's car."

Tori's heart melted at the gentle way Levi carried her daughter. She wanted to cry and scream with relief that her baby girl had been returned unharmed but first she needed to touch her. Nothing mattered at the moment except holding her in her arms.

"I'll take her," she whispered hoarsely.

"Are you sure? I kind of don't want to let her go."

Tori blinked at Levi's statement. Had she heard him correctly? This situation was messing with her head. Still, she reached for her daughter and carefully pulled her from Levi's embrace. Hannah stirred but didn't wake up. "She must be really tired. Are you sure she's okay?" Before Levi answered she buried her face in Hannah's cloud of hair and inhaled. The sweet scent of sugar and childhood innocence assaulted her brain.

"She's definitely okay. Half way home she regaled me with all the details of her day at her father's hotel. Apparently he let her play at the pool and eat junk food all day so she was in heaven."

Her heart squeezed. She hadn't considered that Bill would be nice to her the whole time. Instead she'd assumed the worst. Her stomach cramped. She brushed the hair from her daughter's face and touched the baby soft skin. "I'm a little ashamed now of what I assumed about Bill."

"Don't be. That he treated her well is what saved his life tonight. But that doesn't mean he isn't a dickhead of the first order who deserves everything he gets."

Tori's head shot up. "What the hell happened, anyway? What was the point of all this?"

Levi's shoulders sagged and Tori got the idea this wasn't going to be a pretty story.

"Blackmail. What else?"

Her eyes widened and she gripped Hannah tighter. "What could he possibly blackmail me with? The only thing I have worth anything is her."

"I don't have all the details yet. Mason is handling the negotiation and my singular mission was to get Hannah back to you. I think taking her was just a way of getting attention."

She shook her head. "For what? Why does he all of a sudden want Hannah?" Levi lifted his shoulders but she got the distinct impression he knew way more than he was telling her. Besides, he already had a family. She'd learned that the hard way not long after he'd left. Not that she wanted to admit that to Levi right now. Not explaining why she'd never bothered to get a custody agreement still embarrassed her. But Bill had been more than clear that he didn't want anything more to do with her. He claimed there was no absolution for her sins of the past and unfortunately Hannah was tainted because of it.

Bill was fucking nuts. That much she knew better than anyone.

"I think I should go now." Gabe startled her. She'd forgotten all about him the moment she saw her child.

Gabe turned to Levi. "In the future, don't be such a caveman. I know she's yours now and I respect that."

Tori's mouth dropped open in shock. She was most definitely not his. "I think it's probably time for you both to go. I need to get Hannah home and into bed. She's obviously had an exhausting day.

Levi turned to her. "I'm not going anywhere."

SEVENTEEN

Levi fought the impulse to assert himself over Tori while she sulked. That she'd thought for even a minute that he would leave and she'd go home alone made him slightly crazy. He'd thought they'd moved past some of her guards, but apparently the stress and nightmare of Hannah's kidnapping had put them back to square one.

He pulled her car into his driveway and killed the engine. "We had to come here for both our peace of mind. Fortunately, the worst of the renovations have been completed."

She turned and met his gaze and for the umpteenth time he was blown away with her beauty. Unfortunately the look of resignation on her face and lack of response made him both a little angry and voraciously hungry for her. He shouldn't be having those thoughts at the moment but there they were, flaring to life in the cramped front seat.

She took her seatbelt off and emerged from the car while he retrieved Hannah from the back seat. The day had clearly taken a toll on them all but especially on the sweet girl in his arms. She'd barely stirred from house to car to house again.

Inside he headed to the bedroom he'd had prepared

for guests. Tori followed behind and once he deposited his precious cargo onto the bed, he withdrew from the room to give Tori some space.

Levi prowled through the partially renovated house and marveled how much the contractor and his crew had managed in just a few short days. As promised they'd worked nearly around the clock and finished the bedrooms. He peeked into the kitchen to find they'd accomplished a lot there too. After several long minutes, he grew impatient to be with Tori and returned to the guest room to retrieve her. She wasn't there but he found the hall bathroom door closed and locked.

"Catori, open the door." In his head he counted to ten and was about to knock again when she cracked the door open.

"Why are you hiding?"

Instead of denying the truth, she shrugged. Damn she turned him on. Levi realized he needed to get his own head screwed on right and there was only one way to accomplish that.

"Come out here, please."

To her credit she did exactly that, emerging from the confined space. He tried to put himself in her shoes over the last twelve hours. Hannah wasn't even his child and he'd been ready to commit murder to get her back. His emotions had nearly suffocated him and Tori had to have experienced that tenfold.

Still, that didn't mean they had to backpedal on their blossoming relationship. He'd dared to admit to himself that what he was beginning to feel for this woman went beyond a simple D/s connection. They had a chance at something real.

"Do you regret last night now?" Better to be straightforward than to waste time skirting the issue.

"No," she replied softly. "But..."

"But what?" God, was there anything worse than that word when it came to an important conversation? If it was up to him he'd eradicate that word from Tori's vocabulary for the rest of her life.

"But I told you this had to be temporary." She turned away from him. "I'm not going to lie. There was a period last night where hope for more began to develop but you see where that got us."

He hated the fear he heard in her voice. He wanted to take that from her and he needed to show her that today's event did not preclude them from continuing to explore this relationship.

First, he kissed her. He placed his thumbs along her jawline and wrapped the rest of his hands around her neck and pulled her close. That simple touch ignited the simmering heat in his body and he had to have her. He tangled with her tongue as he walked her backwards into his room. He closed and locked the door and before she could protest he pointed to a panel on the wall.

"Whole house intercom system with a built in monitor. Contractor just got it installed." He pulled at her clothes in a flurry of motion until she stood before him naked. "If Hannah so much as mumbles in her sleep, we'll hear it."

Her shoulders visibly relaxed a whopping inch, but at least they no longer hovered near her ears. He stepped back and admired her body. Her nipples were already hard and just right for pinching.

"You're still mine." He let those three little words sink in before he pulled her into his arms and kissed her again. He apparently couldn't keep his hands and lips off her.

"Say it," he insisted. When she hesitated he repeated himself. "Say it."

He could see the internal war waging inside her. He

reached forward and tweaked her left nipple until her mouth formed that delectable little O. "I didn't imagine last night and I know you felt every word you spoke. So don't close up on me now, Catori. Be brave."

She blushed, the red flush creeping from her chest to her face. He really liked the look of red skin on her and that gave him an idea. He sat down on the end of the bed and patted his lap. "Present yourself for a spanking."

She jerked as if he'd hit her. "What?"

He frowned. "You heard me perfectly well. You don't need a punishment yet, but you do need centering and this is what I want. Submit to me, Catori."

This time there was no hesitation. She moved to him slowly and gingerly draped her body across his lap with her ass sticking up at the perfect angle. Holy shit. She wanted this more than he'd thought.

He rubbed his hand across her bottom several times to warm her up before he leaned close and whispered in her ear. "If you need to come you have permission to do so."

She whimpered.

Levi sat up and spanked her. Hard. The sting of his open hand hitting her smooth flesh vibrated through his body. The sounds of the slaps were music to his ears as were the whimpers flowing from her mouth. With each successive blow he saw her demeanor change through tell tale physical signs. Her skin turned pink, sweat popped out on her arms and legs and she wriggled restlessly.

When her ass flamed bright red and gorgeous he stopped spanking her and dipped a finger into her. The white hot heat and flowing moisture between her legs made his world tilt.

A low growl built inside his chest.

He pulled her to her feet and without letting go of her waist he stood and flipped her around so her back was to his front. With slight pressure on her head he pushed her torso down on to the bed, effectively lining up her sex at the perfect angle for his possession. And that's what this had to be. The need to reassert his Dominance drove him to this point and he'd see it through whenever necessary.

"As my submissive what do you want? Right now at this very moment."

Her words were surprisingly clear. "To give you anything you want." She took a breath before she continued, "I need to please *you*."

Her admission broke him. He pushed her legs farther apart and then quickly freed his cock. It made him almost dizzy to think of her lying wide open and willing to do whatever it took to make him happy. His body screamed for this.

"Being inside you pleases me." He rested his hard erection at the juncture of her thighs and waited as long as he could stand it. "This is me and you, Catori. Dominant and submissive, friends and family. That is what we are. Now tell me this is mine." He edged a finger along side his nestled erection and pushed it inside her.

This woman he'd only known a short time was quickly becoming the woman of his dreams. The woman he needed to claim more than air. The insanity of that aside, she amazed him.

"Say it," he prodded, his finger rubbing her sensitive tissue.

"Oh God, it's true okay?"

He smiled despite himself. Her adorable reluctant admission meant far more to him than some automatic agreement in the heat of the moment.

"Now can we fuck before I go mad?"

Levi thrust into her, his thickness forging through her tight channel in one smooth move. He gave her as long as he could stand to adjust before he started pounding into her.

It took all of thirty seconds for him to realize he wasn't going to last. He hooked his arm around her middle and slipped his finger over her clit. He fucked her with hard, sure strokes that pushed her deeper into the mattress and drove them both quickly to the edge.

"Oh hell. Harder," she cried.

Levi changed his angle slightly and drove into her with more force than ever. He dropped down over her back and plowed into her. "Come for me, Catori. Do it now!" he commanded.

Like a flash fire she exploded and her inner muscles sucked at his dick. Unable to resist the lure of his amazing woman, he switched to short digs designed to brush her G-spot. The moment she screamed his name he joined her and came inside her, continuing to pump long after he'd gone dry before he collapsed over her.

After a short recovery period he reluctantly withdrew from her, hissing as he lost the tight heat of her flesh. While she laid there seemingly unable to move he cleaned them up and then tucked her into bed with her head cradled on his shoulder and their legs entwined. She definitely needed some rest before he woke her for more.

***

Tori woke to just enough hazy light filtering into the space from the wall of windows in front of her so she could see across the room. The sun would rise soon. For a moment she laid there disoriented and unable to breathe very well with whatever lay across her chest.

A look down revealed that she was still in bed with Levi after he'd fucked her near to death. She smothered a giggle. She was now taking perverse pleasure in using the word fuck at every opportunity that suited her.

Sore and extremely satisfied she slipped from under

his arm and reached for her clothes. She wanted to check on Hannah before she woke. Her little girl may not realize the ordeal she'd gone through the day before but it was an experience that Tori would never forget and she needed the reassurance only touching her daughter could bring her.

She crept into the spare bedroom and found her still sound asleep and sprawled across the bed. Her long dark curls were fanned out along the pink pillow and a stuffed animal was clenched in her arms. It was then Tori realized that the room was no ordinary guest room. It had been painted a lovely shade of pale pink and decorated with a strong slant to the feminine side. There were a pile of stuffed animals artfully arranged in the corner and a small child-sized table and chairs with an assortment of crayons and coloring books. Her daughter's favorites, in fact.

Her heart lurched. Had Levi had this room prepared specially for Hannah? She felt bad that he'd gone to that extent to make her daughter feel comfortable. Curious about what else had been completed, she snuck from the room and wandered through the open concept living room and dining room. She barely recognized the place from her previous visit and marveled at the amazing job the contractor and decorators had done.

The lure of the kitchen called to her baker's heart. She couldn't wait to see the transformation in there. The progress stunned her. The kitchen space had been doubled, the new walls completed and the cabinets installed. Even without countertops or appliances she could easily envision what the complete room would look like.

It would be a cook's dream. She counted the three carved out wall niches for ovens and gaped. A baker's dream as well. She imagined when all the work was done the whole house would be a dream house. Maybe even *the* dream house.

That thought halted her on the spot.

The pink bedroom, the spa-like master suite and a baker's dream kitchen. Her gut began to ache. Who in the hell had Levi designed this house for? It looked nothing like a bachelor pad was supposed to. It looked like the perfect place for a family.

Her heart seized.

He'd done this for her.

No fucking way.

Way.

She shook her head. This couldn't be happening. Not again.

Bill had done almost this very thing. He'd come in when she was at her most vulnerable and taken advantage. He'd discovered her weaknesses and exploited them. He'd even claimed what he thought was his and then when she'd finally gotten comfortable years later, he pulled the rug out from under her.

Tori backed away and headed for the bedroom. She grabbed her cell phone and clothes and went into the bathroom. She typed out a text to Josie telling her where she was and asked her to come and get her quickly. Her friend responded right away. *Ok. On my way. Expect explanation and lots of coffee.* Tori thanked her stars for such a good friend.

While she finished dressing, she did everything not to look at the big beautiful man who'd played her body like a freaking conductor. One look and she'd start having second thoughts. Her body would betray her and she'd end up in bed with him again. She shoved her feet into her shoes and went on the hunt for her keys. Once she had everything together she'd retrieve Hannah and they'd hightail it home.

In her search she found some paper and a pen and started to write a note to Levi.

Dear Levi,

Thank you for helping me get Hannah back, you can't imagine how grateful I am. However, I think you've gotten the wrong impression of me and my daughter. From the looks of your house you've made a lot of assumptions. Hannah and I are not a ready made to fulfill your desperate need for an instant family. You should know better than anyone it doesn't work like that. It CAN'T work like that. Bill took advantage of me to suit his selfish fantasies for family and I simply won't go through that again. Hannah and I both deserve better than that.

Please don't follow me or come to my house, my mind is made up and I won't risk my daughter's heart or mine. She already thinks you set the moon and the stars and I fear the truth would crush her.

You have a family. Be happy with them, you deserve that.

Tori

She threw the few items she'd brought with her in Josie's waiting car and then went back in the house for Hannah. Tori's heart pounded so loud and heavy in her chest, she expected it to wake Levi at any moment. Hannah stirred and mumbled something about Mr. Levi.

"He's sleeping, honey. Let's keep quiet and not wake him, okay?"

Her daughter nodded and gave her a sweet smile before she wrapped her arms around her mother's neck.

"Hi, Aunt Josie." Hannah squealed when they got out to the car.

"Hey, sweet pea. Come on let's go get some pancakes at the diner."

"Yes!" Hannah high-fived her and buckled her belt. When Josie backed her car out of the driveway and headed home, the flood of tears threatened to fall and Tori pressed her thumbs to her eye sockets in an attempt to stop them.

"You okay? Headache? Maybe a S.E.X. hangover?" Josie spelled out.

"What I have is all your fault," Tori whispered. "Three-night stand my ass. I'm going to kill you for putting notions like that into my head."

Josie laughed as they sped away. "We'll see..."

EIGHTEEN

Mason walked into his usual private dining room and office-away-from-the-office and glanced around. He'd purposely arrived well before his reporter was due for their meeting. He'd spent the night trying to work through all the angles of Bill Bennett's blackmail scheme and so far had no solution that pleased him. The little shithead had them all by the balls. Somehow he'd gathered enough information over the years to piece together some of his lineage. He'd yet to identify all of the children associated with the charity but he had enough to cause irreparable damage if he chose to go public with it.

He sat down at his computer and pressed a series of buttons. Many of the financials he'd been tracking lately popped onto the screen. He wasn't an idiot, he'd known this day could become a reality and had worked the last ten plus years trying to diversify and free the family fortune from its conservative ties. Still a lot of money remained tied up in businesses that his father's church had supported and vice versa. A few of them had even gone public in recent years. The scandal of their former church leader's true beliefs could still plunge several of the companies into financial ruin.

And then there was Nina. She'd been harder to handle than even Levi. When he'd signed over a small fortune to her when she turned twenty-one, she'd lost her mind and donated every cent to charity. He'd sent her to therapy. Whatever happened that night, his little sister wouldn't talk about it and it was clear it haunted her. Mason sighed. It had taken years and a small cafe she built on her own from the ground up to help her flourish.

Now Bill Bennet was pushing them to the threshold of ruination and there were simply too many risks to have that much attention turned on them. A reporter here and there he could handle. The mass of the press corps digging through all of their backgrounds would eventually break them. Nothing was foolproof.

Levi had offered his share of the inheritance to get the slimeball off their back, but it hadn't been enough. The fucker's greed knew no bounds and ultimately to meet his demands they'd have to pull funding from other secret siblings. An option Mason simply couldn't stomach. Most of those kids were young and deserved their support now more than ever. Especially if their identities got revealed.

"Mr. Sinclair, your guest has arrived. Shall I show her in?" One of the pretty red-headed waitresses poured him a cup of coffee and stood close, waiting for his instructions. Normally a sweet submissive such as her would have caught his eye. But not since Rebecca Adams had entered his life. Since then, she'd never been far from his mind. Even though she represented quite a bit of danger to his family, he'd still become entranced. He wanted to know her better.

"Yes, please show her in." The woman disappeared and Mason's attention returned to the financials on the screen. It was an impossible monetary puzzle. Sacrifice the financial stability for dozens of people or watch one of his employees and Levi's new woman lose everything in the court of law. Bennett had alluded to some pretty salacious secrets on Ms. Ford's part and he didn't doubt she had something to hide. The few times they'd interacted at the club he'd recognized the fearful look of a kindred soul. For that reason alone he'd kept his distance from her or he'd be tempted to pry from her whatever she didn't want people to know. He hoped she came clean with Levi soon.

The tap tap of feminine heels clicking against the marble floors caught his attention. He looked up to find Rebecca striding toward him. Her beautiful blonde curls bounced in rhythm with her steps, but it was the long column of her neck that drew most of his attention. Her delicate skin always appeared translucent and many times he'd imagined that same skin between her thighs. His cock throbbed just thinking about it. He closed his laptop and watched her walk toward him. He had a proposition for her that he prayed she said yes too. He felt certain it offered a solution they'd both find rewarding.

"Mr. Sinclair, I appreciate you seeing me." She held out her hand.

He stood and instead of shaking her hand he gripped it gently and brought it to his lips. "It is my pleasure." He placed a soft kiss just about her delicate knuckles and held her to him for a few seconds longer than would be considered appropriate. Her eyes opened and her nose flared. Her lips parted slightly. It all added up to the scenario he'd intended for today's meeting.

"Please have a seat." He waited for her to take a chair before he resumed his position behind the desk. "I imagine you're wondering why I've finally asked you here after all the turned down requests for an interview."

She dipped her head, "Yes, while I'm extremely grateful, I am curious as to what changed your mind."

"Fair enough." He picked up the remote control sitting on his desk and pointed it to the wide flat screen hanging on the nearby wall. "This is what changed my mind." He turned it on and kept his eyes trained on Rebecca. He'd already watched the surveillance tapes too many times to be considered normal. The images of her sitting and observing in Purgatory Club had kept him awake many nights. Much like she sat now with her back ramrod straight and her legs crossed across her knees showing off a criminal amount of thigh drove him mad. She uncrossed and recrossed them right in front of him.

After a few moments she turned to him. "I don't get it. What's the point of showing me in the club? I didn't exactly try to hide my presence or my intentions to get an interview."

He leaned forward and captured her gaze. "It's not just your presence that I found so remarkable. It's the way your body responded to what you were watching. In this video in particular, you were watching a submissive be disciplined by her Dom for breaking one of his rules. If I remember correctly, it was a whipping by belt."

To Rebecca's credit, her face remained passive, although the flare of heat in her eyes gave her away. "And your point?" she asked.

"Let's not waste each other's time. I believe you came here for a story but you've stayed here for something more."

"I have no idea what you're referring to," she denied. She sat back in her chair and her eyes shifted away. "I've made no secret of my interest in Purgatory Club and its mysterious owner." She'd implied many times that either he or Gabe owned it, but she had no proof one way or another. His attorney had made sure of that. The original ownership between he, Tucker and Levi had been hidden among a maze of international shell corporations. It was highly doubtful anyone could prove ownership to an individual level.

"I disagree, Miss Adams. You reacted to the scene

in that video and many more. It is as if you wish that you were the one on the table experiencing submission."

"You've been watching me that much? Why?"

He liked the way her mind worked. Instead of continuing her denial about her intentions, she'd turned the tables back to him, trying to make him the focus of this conversation. Little did she know he'd prepared for any argument.

"It's my job as a Dom to notice a submissive in need. It's like a siren call that cannot be denied. There are very few Doms in Purgatory who haven't noticed. Most, of course know you are a reporter and are inclined to keep their distance. I am, however, not one of them."

She swallowed, the muscles in her gorgeous neck tightening. "What's the point? I'm only here to do a job. I'm not looking for anything else."

"I don't believe you. You can deny it until your face turns blue and I will still know that a submissive yearning to be explored sits in the chair in front of me." He stood and walked around his desk and stopped at the back of her chair. "Look at the woman on the screen, Miss Adams. Watch her eyes so full of naked emotion take in the scene she can't turn away from. See the perspiration dot across her forehead as her body heat rises with her arousal. And watch her hands grip the sides of the chair each time the belt lands on the naked backside of the other woman."

Mason reached for the skin he'd ached to touch and traced his finger from her jaw to the dip of her collarbone. "I have a proposition for you, Miss Adams. Become my submissive and let me train you to discover the depth of your submission." The only sound he heard was both their heavy breathing. "And in exchange I will give you the information you seek. At least as much as I'm able." He reached for the contract he'd prepared for this meeting and pushed it in front of her. If you're willing to abide by all the rules and stipulations in this document I believe we could experience a mutually beneficial relationship, Miss Adams."

Before Rebecca could respond, the door behind him burst open and Gabe's voice filled the room.

"Sorry to interrupt you, Mason. But you need to turn the news on *now*."

Mason glared at Gabe for ten seconds before the words sunk in. His friend had interrupted at the worst possible moment.

Gabe looked at the television and the surveillance tape they'd been watching and then looked between them. His face softened momentarily. "I'm truly sorry, but this is an emergency. Tucker's mother has called a press conference and I don't think you want to miss it." He glanced at his watch. "It started thirty seconds ago."

NINETEEN

Turn the TV on NOW.

Levi stared at the text message from Mason and shook his head. He could always count on his brother to send only urgent and necessary communications. His flair for the dramatic was uncanny. He considered ignoring it in favor of another beer. Since Tori had left last week he didn't care much what his brothers or anyone else had to say. He only wanted to hear from her. Still, the curiosity over Mason's command niggled at the back of his mind and he found himself reaching for the remote control.

The television powered on and an older and still very beautiful version of Tucker's mother filled the screen. "Oh shit." Levi stood up and moved closer while pressing the up button on the volume. She stood at a podium with several people in suits behind her that he didn't recognize. He searched the crowd around her, surprised to see no sign of Tucker. What the hell was going on?

"So for those just tuning in," an offscreen reporter's voice broke in. "Mrs. Savannah Lewis, wife to deceased televangelist Reverend Lewis and mother to the notorious artist and heir of his estate, Tucker Lewis, has just announced that much of her husband's religious empire has been based upon lies and in some states, fraud."

Levi's mouth gaped open. Holy shit. His head swam with all the implications of her taking this information public. The people that would be affected. How was this happening?"

The reporters voice faded and Mrs. Lewis began speaking again. "As I've said previously, I had no clue about my husband's extra curricular activities inside and outside the church. The fact he'd fathered many children outside our marriage did not come to light until the day he died. After his death there were rumors brought to my son's attention that he'd married other women in different states but as far as I know none of those claims were ever substantiated."

That's because Mason swept them under the proverbial rug with a shitload of money specifically for that purpose.

Reporters tried firing questions at Mrs. Lewis but she didn't respond. God, none of this made sense. The last he'd heard about Tucker's mother was that she sat in a mental institution not far from Charlotte where she'd refused to speak for over a decade. None of which fit with the woman's seeming perfectly sane image filling the screen. She stood tall and spoke with conviction, the only hint that something wasn't quite right was in her eyes. She looked unfocused and unseeing as if she'd chosen a spot at the back of the room to focus on and couldn't or wouldn't look elsewhere. It came off a little too mechanical.

"I have no idea if he broke any federal or state laws. But as far as I'm concerned he broke God's laws in the most blatant and vicious way a man can and for that he was punished."

The crowd exploded and Levi felt the blood drain from his face. After several long minutes of the men in suits trying to contain the chaos, Mrs. Lewis was able to continue.

"I know what you all want to know and as I said when I started this press conference, the time has come to clear the air and put things right. Reverend Lewis, my husband, *was* punished for all of his crimes. I know this because I'm the one who punished him and now one of his bastard sons is trying to turn a madman's quest into his own by following in his father's footsteps under the guise of religion. He must be stopped!"

The barely restrained chaos busted free. So many flash bulbs went off, Tucker's mother disappeared from the screen in a wash of bright white light. She was jerked away from the podium by one of the men in suits behind her and the camera lens widened, giving him and the rest of the world a good look at Mrs. Lewis being ushered away with several uniformed police officers behind them.

The reporter's voice returned and all Levi heard was a constant buzz droning in his head. Nearly everything he'd spent his adult life running from had just been exposed on public television in a matter of seconds.

The image of his own mother's grief-stricken face when he'd informed her of his father's death became front and center in his mind. She'd fallen to the ground wailing like a wounded beast and Levi had never been so scared in his life. He'd tried to console her and nothing worked. Nothing. When she'd picked up the gun he'd tried to stop her, but he wasn't smart enough or fast enough.

Her death had been all his fault.

It felt like someone had sliced him open and his guts were spilling out. Just like his men in Afghanistan. Ambushed because he'd fallen for fake intel. Him. His fault.

Just like Hannah's kidnapping had been because of him. If he hadn't bulldozed his way into Tori's life, Bennett wouldn't have had any reason to ever come after Hannah. Tori had suffered because of him.

Tori.

Tall, beautiful and so damned perfect for him. He hadn't stopped thinking about her since she pushed him away and he couldn't let it go. He'd fought the need to go after her for her sake until they'd cleared things up with Bennett the bastard. He only wanted the best for her, but now everything was spinning out of control and all he could focus on was Tori.

His stomach tightened and his fists clenched. Something hot and unbelievably sharp filled his mind. Tori. Hunger. He had to go.

Levi dropped the remote and ran from his house with barely enough thought to remember his keys and phone. His thoughts were running away from him and he couldn't keep up. His world had tilted and he needed Tori with a fierceness he couldn't explain. With her he could regain enough control to figure out what to do next.

He was already half way down the long driveway on his bike when it dawned on him he didn't know where she was. He stopped and pulled the phone from his pocket, tapping out a text.

Urgent: Where are you?

Seconds ticked by agonizingly slow as he waited for her to answer. If she didn't respond then he'd methodically search the town until he found her. His brain had locked onto Tori as the one sane thing around him and there was no other choice for him but to find her. See her. Touch her. Of course it didn't make sense considering she'd told him that she and Hannah would not be his ready made family. Still, his mind rebelled. Mine. Find her. The brutal, almost painful need overrode all common sense.

I'm at Nina's Cafe. What's up?

The relief he'd hoped for at her response didn't come. The hunger for his Catori consumed him. It no longer mattered whether it made sense or if it was right or wrong. It just was.

He dropped the phone in his pocket and roared down the road.

Nothing else mattered besides getting to Tori.

***

Tori stared at her phone, unsure if she was ready to talk to Levi again. But she doubted he would say it was urgent if it wasn't. So she'd answered and now she sat numbly waiting for him to text again.

"Who was that?"

Tori cocked her head and smirked at Josie. They'd come to Nina's cafe to pick her up for their first weekly night out. Now they were just waiting for her to finish up waiting on a few last customers before they could leave.

"What did he say? Does he want to see you?" Josie asked.

"I don't know. He asked where I was and said it was urgent but so far he hasn't said anything else."

"Do I get to tell you I told you so yet? I knew he wasn't going to be a three night stand kind of guy for you. He'll be back."

"That doesn't mean I'm going to rush into a relationship with him just because I fit the bill of the ready made family he's looking for. Like I told him, that's bullshit."

"You have got to be one of the most stubborn women I have ever met. You've got one of the hottest men on the planet, who by your own admission is the most amazing sex you've ever had, and you're just going to cut him loose before even giving something more a chance. That makes no damn sense. Why not at least talk to him again?"

Tori didn't want to think about the last time she'd been with Levi, if she did the stupid tears would return. She hadn't confided to even Josie how much walking away from him that morning had devastated her. Heat crept from her chest to her face and she realized she was blushing.

Ridiculous

It was impossible to fall for someone after just a few days. Not that the sadness inside Levi didn't pull at her like a magnet to metal. He definitely deserved to fall in love and have the family he ached for, but after the man pulled her submissive side to the surface she realized she'd been doing a disservice to her family by ignoring her needs. Although the idea of seeking a different Dom made her stomach hurt. She'd experienced amazing love in her young life and she wanted Levi to find someone he could feel that way about rather than settling for her and Hannah because they were available.

That meant it was up to her to move on. She'd have to start dating. Which meant so would Levi...

"Are you even listening to me, young lady?"

Tori jerked from her thoughts and faced Josie. "Kind of. I'm a little distracted."

Josie laughed. "Ya think? If you were any farther away I'd need a satellite phone to reach you."

"I'm sorry it's just been one hell of a week. But I'm trying, I really am." She hadn't heard much more about Bennett other than a couple of email messages from Mason letting her know that he was still working on negotiations and that Levi had already provided instructions to pay any price. None of it made any sense. Why were they working so hard on her behalf?

She wondered if Bill had somehow found out about who the real owners of Purgatory were and was using that information to extort money from them. She'd been on pins and needles waiting for the subject of Seth to come up. Bill had once lorded the truth about her fiancé over her to keep her in line when she'd discovered his wife and to her shame she'd allowed it. She doubted he was the kind of man who would keep her secrets if it meant he could profit from them.

"So where are we going to go tonight?" Nina had stopped by their table just in time to hear Tori's question.

"I want to go to Purgatory."

"What?" Both Tori and Josie whipped around to face Nina. "Why? I thought Tucker's kinky love life creeped you out?"

Nina shrugged. "I just love torturing him. That doesn't mean all this talk about whips and chains really turns me off. A girl has a right to be curious."

Tori stared at her in shock.

"Hot damn!" Josie exclaimed. "It's been forever since I've been allowed to get my freak on."

Tori shook her head. "So much for one normal friend," she quipped.

"Aww, you thought I was normal? Aren't you sweet." Before Tori could respond to Nina she got flagged down by one of her customers. "Be right back. Why don't you have some pie and then I'll be ready to blow this joint. She rushed off and Tori watched her for a minute, talking and joking with the two men at the other table. It was really hard to think of her as Levi's sister. There were simply too many changes all at once to take in.

"I'll grab the pie. Be right back." She jumped from the booth and headed around the counter.

"I want apple." Josie yelled. She waved at her friend and grabbed some plates before she dug into the pie case.

Purgatory. How could she go there and not think about the amazing scene between her and Levi next door. Or the night he'd interrupted her shift as one of the club's pro Dommes. As much as she'd been afraid to admit it, he'd changed something in her that night. With the first click of the cuff being locked around her wrist her world had tilted and something inside her shifted. He'd seen what no one since Seth had seen and he'd had to look way beyond the surface to find it.

A lump formed in her throat. Was she kidding herself about Levi? When it came to him she had a hard time being objective. If he'd texted her back and asked to meet her would she have said no? Doubtful. Since she'd walked away from him her body and mind had clamored for him almost non-stop. He'd given her enough of a taste of what it was like to submit to him and despite any thoughts about what a bad idea it was, she wanted a whole lot more.

Her only saving grace at this point had been his restraint. One word from him and she was ready to jump. Kneeling and begging sounded good too. She placed two slices of apple on the plates and then disappeared into the small cooler for some whipped cream. Spray can in hand, a different use for the confection came to mind. She already knew Levi had a thing for pie with his whipped cream, how about her and whipped cream?

Heat surged to her core at the thought. It was clear she'd developed a serious weakness to a certain tattooed bad boy. Her heart ached thinking about him.

She stopped in mid motion. He'd fallen for the idea of what she represented. A family. And she'd fallen in love with the man. The perfect, stubborn, demon-ridden, sweet, risk-taking, hard headed man.

Now what? She couldn't take back what she'd said. Just because she had feelings didn't dismiss the truth about how he felt. Seeing him taking another submissive would kill her.

What was she supposed to--

"Catori."

She froze at the sound of her name. Her blood surged and her body went from hot to burning up in flames in 2.5 seconds.

She turned to investigate as did everyone else in the small restaurant. But she didn't need to see his face to know who. She'd recognize that Dom voice anywhere.

Levi had come for her.

"Catori," he repeated. Her sex squeezed as her name from his lips made her body tingle. As usual. She couldn't remember another time in her life when she'd ever loved her full name as much as she did now.

She squeezed her eyes shut and counted to five. That's all she could take before she opened them again, this time taking note of more than his mouth. Like the first time she'd seen him, he appeared disheveled. Instead of dirt and grime it was clothes that looked like they'd been slept in and bloodshot eyes that looked like he hadn't closed them in days.

"Levi." It's all she could think to say and she was amazed she got that much out. He'd seemed sad when she'd walked out on him before but this looked worse, much worse. He looked devastated. Something had gone terribly wrong. "What's wrong?"

She rushed forward. "Did something happen?" He simply stared at her and this time she got a glimpse she didn't fully understand. His eyes roamed over her like they'd devour her if he could. A quick glance down and she got a whole nother level of understanding. He needed her.

"Come with me."

She glanced at Nina who nodded her head. Tori grabbed Levi's hand and pulled him back to the office.

The moment they crossed the threshold the air around her shifted and Levi slammed the door shut behind them a second before he flipped her against it. He ground into her hip to hip and she whimpered. "I wanted to talk. Now I can't. Strip."

His inability to put together full sentences was all the warning she needed. She pulled her shirt over her head and flung it away. She reached for her bra and he shoved her hands away. "Mine," he growled.

He snapped open the front bra enclosure and exposed her breasts. His hands cupped them both and he groaned. He bent forward and sucked one and then the other into his mouth. Moisture pooled between her legs. Since she had no idea what happened to get him like this she was helpless to do anything but enjoy the moment. His movements were rough and she loved it. She arched her chest forward and moaned when he bit a trail from each breast to her mouth. From there he kissed her hard, robbing her of breath and the last bit of common sense she still clung to.

She kissed him back with every emotion that had left her adrift for days. He pressed harder and she met him thrust for thrust with her tongue. Need arched between them as they fought to crawl inside each other. Levi grabbed at the bottom of her skirt and lifted it over her hips and she thanked God she'd forgone her usual skin tight jeans. If she had to stop to get undressed before he touched her she'd go mad for sure.

He broke free from her mouth. "I can't stop thinking about being inside you, Catori. You've ruined me." His fingers curled around the delicate lace of her bikini panties and ripped.

"Now you've ruined another pair of my panties," she groaned.

"Then don't wear them." He murmured into her hair. "Every time I find them on you I *will* rip them off."

His sensual threat sent a shiver racing down her spine. She refused to consider the implication of his words. He cupped her bottom and lifted her off the ground and wrapped her legs around his waist. They spun around and he placed her on the desk. Papers and whatever else covered the surface got shoved to the side. The incongruity of their location would have struck her as funny if not for the desperate need coursing through her. His out of control animalistic actions did crazy things to her head.

He pulled away only long enough to free his cock. As if his life depended on it, he came over her and thrust in her; hard. She gasped at the sudden sensation of being stretched beyond capacity. It took her breath away. Levi buried his head in her neck and shuddered underneath her hands still gripping his shoulders.

"I need to make this good for you. I want to take my time and watch you come over and over again but I can't." He withdrew to the tip and shoved inside her again. She cried out, oblivious to whether anyone heard her or not. Had he ever been so deep inside her? Had anyone?

He lifted his head and their gazes met as he set a steady paced rhythm of deep strokes that left her little ability to do anything other than feel. He pinned her down with that lake blue gaze she couldn't escape from. Emotion she recognized and didn't want to put a name to filled her heart and throat until she couldn't breathe. The thin veneer of civility she'd been desperate to hold onto crumbled away as she raised her hips to meet his thrusts.

Sweat slicked their skin, muscles strained in his neck. In this moment, there was nothing between them but this. No secrets, no preconceived notions and no way to deny she'd fallen in love with him almost from the moment she'd watched her child hand over the picture she'd drawn of their home. The innocence of childhood had seen through this man's exterior to his heart and she'd known even when Tori didn't. His heart ached with loneliness.

"Catori," he whispered against her lips. "Mine."

Tears filled her eyes. She couldn't speak.

He must have understood because he readjusted his angle and drove in to her repeatedly until she flew apart around him. "Levi," she screamed, her nails digging into his shoulders. She wanted him to fall with her and he did. Completely and irrevocably hers.

TWENTY

Tori took her time pulling her clothes on while Levi attempted to put Nina's office back together. She was still a little stunned by what had just happened between them and she needed a moment or five hundred to get her head on straight. He seemed to do that a lot to her.

Her body and her head had literally just waged an epic battle against each other and she still wasn't sure who'd come out victorious. She'd been so resolute when she told Levi that she didn't think they should see each other again until he came to terms with his demons.

Hypocrite.

She cringed. Her hang ups were every bit as much of a barrier as his were. She'd have to suck it up and confide in him like she'd tried with Bill and pray the outcome turned out better. They simply couldn't go forward until they started talking.

"Levi," she started.

He turned to her, a sharp look in his eyes. "Don't you dare tell me this was a mistake," he warned. "Even after everything, I still consider you my submissive and if you insist on reducing what happened just now to something trivial, then you and I are headed home right now for a proper scene. One that will start with a punishment session the likes of which you will never forget."

Her stomach jerked and even though he'd leveled her moments ago with arguably the best orgasm of her life, the thought of another formal scene with him excited her. In fact her body started a slow burn of anticipation.

"Actually I was going to suggest we talk."

He stared at her for a long moment. She felt him trying to see inside her head and half expected he saw everything despite her attempt to maintain her secrets.

"I--"

A loud knock landed on the door. "Is it safe to come in there yet?" Nina asked through the wood. At that moment Tori realized how much sound carried inside this building and she felt a blush creeping up her face.

"Sure," Levi grunted.

The door swung wide and Nina popped her head in. She took in the scene inside her tiny office and cringed. "Oh. My. God. I now have to burn that desk and everything on it. Couldn't you two be normal and just get a room?"

Tori blushed from her toes to her head. "You heard?"

"Oh, honey, everyone within a five mile radius probably heard you screaming." The grin on Nina's face made Tori want to run and hide.

"I'm sorry," she started.

"I'm not. I had a feeling warning off Levi would be about as effective as yelling when you see a bear in the woods. I just want to know if we are still going to Purgatory? I'm ready to blow this place and go have some fun. Some of us didn't just get screaming orgasm lucky."

Tori started to open her mouth to say something when she caught a glimpse of the storm brewing across Levi's face. Uh oh.

"You were going to Purgatory?"

"I—Uh—" She didn't know what to say here. Things had definitely just changed between them.

Nina wrinkled her nose at them. "Is this that Dom/sub thing where you get to go all cavemen on her for doing what she wanted to do?"

"Nina, if you weren't my sister I'd probably recommend you need to learn a thing or two about submission. Your knowledge is appalling. However, under no circumstances are you going anywhere near that place tonight."

Tori's eyes widened and her eyebrows raised. Was he crazy? Nina was about to eat him for lunch.

"What did you just say?" Nina sputtered. "I need to learn a thing or two? That's rich coming from you Mr. Bad Ass Biker I Keep Things All Bottled Up so no one can help me bullshit."

The scowl on Levi's face deepened and Tori struggled with whether to step between them or let the siblings duke this out. She had a feeling whatever was going on had been coming for a while.

"Me? ME? You're so uptight it must hurt like hell to be carrying around such a big stick. Just because you've chosen to cover up everything with sarcasm and a smart mouth doesn't make you any better than the rest of us."

Tori's mouth dropped open.

"At least I don't try to fake it through life through some bullshit kink as an excuse for your fucked up life."

Tori felt her face flame as their insults escalated to the ridiculous. They'd both gone waay to far. "I think you're both full of shit when it comes to each other," she interjected. "Why don't you just admit that whatever happened all those years ago tore you apart and you don't know how to fix it? Then maybe you both can discuss it like normal adults." She turned to Nina specifically. "Please don't throw kink and BDSM into whatever it is that has made you hurt. You'll never understand how special and exciting submission can be if you can't get past those preconceived notions of yours."

It was Nina's turn to stare open-mouthed.

"Well, I'm right," Tori insisted. "It was your idea to go to Purgatory tonight and I doubt it was because you crave their dance floor."

Nina clamped her mouth shut and turned away. Tori imagined the tears forming in her friend's eyes and guilt began crowding her mind. She started to reach for her. Instead Levi cut her off at the pass and he rested his hands on Nina's shoulders instead.

"We've really fucked this up, Nina. Our plan didn't work out so well did it? We should have stood up for you back then and I'm sorry we didn't."

"We were kids, Levi. It's more my fault than anyone else's that you had to leave. If not for that night... I ruined your life."

Tori watched them thoroughly confused. What the hell were they talking about? What had happened?

Before anyone got a chance to speak again the door crashed open and both Nina and Tori gasped. Mason and Gabe filled the doorway with matching broad shoulders and deep scowls.

"You've heard?"

"Oh God, what now?" Nina didn't look like a woman who could take any more bad news but judging from the concern now etched on all three men's faces, Tori's hope for peace between Levi and Nina disappeared in a puff of invisible smoke.

"Tucker's mother held a press conference this afternoon. She confessed everything on live national television. The press is having a field day and they're looking for you."

Nina blanched; her knees buckled. If not for a quick

witted Gabe who swept in and caught her, she would have crashed to the floor. The reverent way he spoke and touched her friend gave her pause. Was something going on there?

"Great way to drop the news, Mason. Fucking bull in china shop." Levi crossed to Tori and pulled her into his arms. "I should probably get you home before anyone sees us together."

"Too late for that. Two news vans pulled in right behind us," Gabe informed them.

Tori looked up at Levi. "What is going on? Did you guys rob a bank or something?" she asked.

"If only. A bank heist would be infinitely easier to explain than this cluster fuck."

"Someone needs to tell me something. I don't understand any of what's going on. Why is the press here and why does Nina need to hide from them?"

Levi glanced at Mason and he shrugged. "Might as well." He checked his watch. "It's only a matter of time now before the connection to Bennett is revealed."

Levi glared at him. "What did you do?"

"What? It's not my mother who spilled the beans on national television. But since I had a reporter standing next to me when she did, I saw a short window of opportunity to crush the house of Bill Bennett before he caused any more harm. He should be getting a visit from the local police department any minute."

Alarm shot through Tori. *Hannah.* "Where's my baby?"

"Relax," Mason soothed. "I already checked in with your grandmother and all is well. She's spoiling your daughter as we speak and the guards are watching them both like hawks."

Tori relaxed a fraction. "Then someone needs to tell me what happened."

Levi wrapped his arm around her waist and pulled her closer. "You're not going to like this," he warned. "But I did it for your own good."

Oh great. Famous last words.

"When I told you that Levi, Tucker, Mason and I were brothers I didn't tell you about the rest."

"The rest?" She felt the sudden pull of tension in her head.

"Our illustrious father did not stop at four children. And I'm not talking about a simple polygamist either. He was a serial breeder who believed that overpopulating his gene pool with male children from different women would gain him more power from God. There are dozens of children out there and Bill Bennett is one of them."

Her hand flew to her mouth. The happy ever after she'd imagined less than thirty minutes ago dissolved in a series of unraveled lies and her own half truths. What had she been thinking?

"Even worse," this time Mason interjected. "Bennett has chosen to carry on in his father's footsteps. I've got evidence of at least six children at various ages with four different women."

"No!" Nina wailed and this time Gabe wasn't fast enough. She collapsed onto the floor in a series of mournful wails.

TWENTY ONE

"It's been two weeks, where do things stand now?" Mason directed the question at all of them. He obviously wanted an update from everyone.

They all sat around the dining table at Tucker's house. They'd moved their meeting from the usual Fire and Ice restaurant to the privacy of his brother's lake front home.

Tucker spoke first. "Very slow progress on the police investigation. They seem to have taken my mother's confession at face value and haven't yet reopened the investigation into the fire. They did pull the fire inspector from the case back in and he confirmed his original report that the fire was accidental."

"At least that's something." Mason made a note on his tablet computer.

"I still can't believe she went public like that. Have you been able to talk to her? Gotten an explanation?"

Tucker hung his head, "Only briefly. Apparently they are determined to establish sound mental health before they proceed and are being cautious about who she spends time with."

"Well, duh. She's been in a mental health facility for

a decade, I'm not even sure why they took her seriously in the first place. No offense intended, bro. It just seems unusual."

"I agree. I did finally get to ask her why the press conference and she refused to answer. The whole damn thing is such a mess."

"Mason looked up from his notes, "I'm working damage control as much as possible. Miss Adams has been most helpful in that regard." Levi took note of the strange expression on his face.

Tucker shook his head. "You're flirting with serious danger with that angle. Why not let the attorneys and publicists handle it? It's what they get paid for."

"You do it your way and I'll do it mine," Mason replied, effectively ending that thread of conversation.

"Why did she lie though?" Levi put the question out there because he knew someone had to. This wasn't over and Tucker's mother had gone well beyond opening a can of worms.

"Are you certain she did?" Tucker looked miserable when he said it. Of course no one wanted to believe she'd actually done it because the alternative was no better. Their options were slim to none.

"We were all there that night and saw what we saw." Mason's jaw tightened. "I'd be a lot happier if Nina would open up."

"She's been traumatized all over again what do you expect? Maybe its better if we let this be the end of it." Levi stood up for her because he wasn't sure anyone else would. The subtle shift in loyalties in the last two weeks had left them all unsettled. Suspicions were flying, investigators were watching them like hawks, and for him the fact he'd only seen Tori once since she walked out with a note had him on the razor's edge.

While he'd been convinced that she'd see past the

ugliness of some aspects of his life and still wanted him, Mason and Tucker had urged him to let her be for a while. If it was meant to be then she deserved the space she asked for. Losing Hannah, even for a day and then finding out it was all connected to her relationship with him had been quite a blow. He'd wanted to fight his brothers on their point, but had ultimately conceded that she did deserve some time to work through finding out Bill was his bastard brother on her own. So he'd stayed away from her house, Nina's cafe and Fire and Ice. Anywhere he might accidentally run into her. He also worked almost around the clock and finished the renovations on his house.

The only thing he'd learned from the separation so far is that the heart didn't grow fonder from time apart, it fucking went ape shit possessive.

"Levi, are you with us?"

He lifted his head and met Mason's gaze. He still wanted to kick his ass half the time, but Tucker had assured him that was normal when it came to family. Even a fucked up one like theirs.

"Yeah, I'm here."

"Still haven't heard from her I take it?" Tucker asked.

He shook his head.

"And it's eating you alive isn't it?" He clapped Levi on the shoulder. "I know exactly what that feels like. Have you figured out why yet?"

"Dare I ask?"

A big ass grin broke out across Tucker's face. "Brother, you're in love. Hopelessly, desperately in love. That makes for one powerful submissive."

Levi looked from Tucker to Mason who simply scowled, and then back to Tucker.

"Only question left is what are you going to do about it now that you know?"

***

Tori pulled her car into her driveway and heaved a sigh of relief. After two weeks off from work, at Gabe's insistence, her first day back had been long and exhausting. Much harder than she'd expected. She'd spent most of her shift worrying that Levi or one of his brothers would come in and she'd have to deal with everything she'd been through right then and there. The sense of impending heartache loomed as she waited for the moment she'd have to face him.

Lucky for her, none of them had made an appearance in Fire & Ice and she didn't have the guts to go look in Purgatory. He'd torn the blinders off about her submission and she couldn't bear to examine why she ached so badly. Since the eye opening night in Nina's office she'd done her level best to put Levi behind her. A feat much easier said than done. The minute she didn't think about him the television would run a salacious story on the suspicious circumstances surrounding the death of Reverend Lewis and the current case against his widow. God she hoped that fifteen minutes of notoriety ended soon. She'd had her fill and it made her ill to think about Levi and his family having to suffer through weeks and maybe months of scandal.

She still saw Nina three times a week when Tori delivered her pies to the cafe, but their friendship had cooled. Or maybe Nina had withdrawn. She looked so sad and Tori didn't have a clue how to help her. The whole situation felt impossible. Even Hannah had gotten huffy with her when she refused to let her see her friend Levi.

But the last thing she needed to have happen would be for her relationship with Seth to somehow make things worse for him. She had to distance herself.

Tori approached the door and spied a white piece of paper taped to the wood. Her shoulders sagged. She was going to break down in tears right here on her porch if another person wanted something from her she didn't have. Even a bill collector.

Except upon examination this note only had three handwritten words each of which filled her with a new sense of dread.

Don't be mad.

Josie

She unlocked the door and stepped inside while trying to brace herself for whatever Josie was up to. It was dark and quiet inside with only the small light above the kitchen stove to illuminate the small space. They must have given up on her and gone to bed. She blew out her breath. Thank goodness. She was too tired to fake it tonight. All she had the energy for was a hot bath before she fell into the bed and tried to sleep again.

Tori stepped toward the hallway when her peripheral vision picked up on something out of the ordinary. She turned and covered her mouth to smother her gasp. Oh. My. God.

Levi was stretched out on her small sofa with his feet hanging over one end and his arm tucked behind his head at the other. In no way, shape or form was her furniture built for a man his size. The even more shocking part was the tiny girl tucked into his side with her hand gathered into his. They were both sound asleep and looked absolutely perfect together. There were pages and pages from Hannah's coloring books strewn across the floor. Some colored by her and other's most likely done by him. If ever she'd imagined a new father for her daughter it would be someone just like him. He'd been damaged in so many ways, but he had an amazing heart and a bond with her daughter.

Tori dropped to her knees and silently wept for what couldn't be. Her heart ached for the Dom, the protector, the friend and the perfect father she knew he could be.

"Catori." His sleep roughened voice called out to her in a low tone.

She turned away from him and frantically wiped the tears from her face. She should have known he would catch her. He was the kind of man who would always know when she needed him. She started to rise.

"Stay there," he ordered, his voice strong even in hushed tones. "I will put Hannah to bed and then we will fix this once and for all." He rose in one fluid motion with her daughter tucked safely in his arms. To him she probably weighed nothing, to her she was growing too big to carry around.

She listened to his soothing tones as he reassured her back to sleep. Was it wrong she ached for him to do the same for her? She shook the thought from her head, stood and quickly gathered the crayons and papers and put them in a neat pile on the island. Tori stared at the floor. Had he actually meant for her to stay in that exact spot on the floor? She hesitated. Dare she? What she was about to do felt a little like teasing the tiger at this point but her tired brain couldn't fight with him right now. Some things would always give her comfort and this was one of them. She removed her shoes and returned to her spot on the carpet with her head down and her arms behind her back. The position thrust her breasts forward. There were simply some things as effortless as riding a bike to her and of all people he would understand.

"Shit." Levi's exclamation startled her. "Do you have any idea how delectable you look right now?" He walked up beside her and threaded his fingers through her hair. She leaned into his leg and took the comfort his touch

LEVI'S ULTIMATUM

allowed.

She didn't know what to expect from him now but the thought of him needing her again had crossed her mind. If he'd come here for a respite from the cruel mess his family was embroiled in, she wouldn't turn him away. Couldn't. She craved him every minute her eyes were open and sometimes even when they weren't. Somehow he'd imprinted on her psyche and it wasn't going away.

"Why are you here?" she asked. If she kept her mind busy with questions maybe she'd avoid blurting out a full confession.

Instead of the expected tug of her hair and the touch from above, he untangled his fingers and slid to the floor in front of her. "I came to ask you," he hesitated and her breath hitched. Whatever it was she couldn't breathe. All the air had been sucked from her lungs. "I came to ask you face to face. Why? I gave you as much time to think through things as I could bear. Now I need to know why."

She blinked. "Why?" she repeated. "Why what?"

His piercing blue eyes zeroed in on her reaction. "Why you are still avoiding me? Until now I was afraid to hear your answer to that question and now I can't live without it."

Still speechless, she couldn't answer. He was afraid?

"No. This isn't right. I'm the one who is a coward."

He reached forward and cupped her face with both hands. "How can you say that? You've been unbelievably brave through more than your fair share of adversity. You deserve more. You *need* more. As do I."

Her heart froze on his last three words. Something about him had changed since she'd first met him and she'd missed it until now. He didn't appear as desolate as he once had. Sad yes. Lost no.

"The last couple of weeks have been rather hellish for my family, but I think some of this coming to light was what we needed. It put several things into perspective and despite what you believe, my feelings for you are very real. Yes, I still want a family and yes, you do come with a ready made one as you so eloquently put it. But that's going to be true no matter what happens in the future. It just so happens I want to be that future."

Tori could hardly believe he'd come to her house, let alone he might have real feelings for her. Except he didn't know the truth and when he did there was a very real chance he'd never look at her the same. Fear of that revulsion seized her heart. She couldn't take it again. Not when that part of her had proved to be so much of who she was. Seth was the first man she'd loved and the one who'd taught her about submission. No matter the circumstances she'd never allow for regret. Those memories were simply a part of her.

"Unless the truth about my family is simply too ugly. I can't deny it's complicated. If we end up together, I'd technically be Hannah's uncle and stepfather." He attempted a small smile and her heart ached for the hell he'd been through already. He didn't deserve more.

Levi was looking at her with huge expectations. She had to say something. The moment had come to tell him the truth and she was starting to sweat. Her stomach churned. There was nothing to do but spit it out and deal with the fallout after. "I haven't been completely honest with you," she said.

Tori hated that small frightened voice that sounded eerily like the one in her head but she forged ahead anyway. "Bill knew the truth and he couldn't take it."

"I am nothing like Bennett. And I am nothing like the man who was technically my biological father."

She shook her head. "That's not what I meant. I only use Bill as a reference because other than my grandmother, no one else knows the truth about what I did.

You already know a little about Seth."

"Your first love and first Dom," his voice had softened with reverence and she wanted to cry with appreciation for the moment.

"Seth was my brother." Levi blinked several times but to his credit he kept his facial expression neutral. "Technically, step brother but I think of his father as my dad so it makes it a little weird in *my* head, let alone everyone else's. My mother was ashamed of me but she managed to tolerate it until Seth died and I found out I was pregnant. She asked me to leave as politely as a mother does when she doesn't want anyone to know the truth, and I came here to stay with my grandmother until I came up with a plan."

"Wait? Are you saying Bill Bennett is not Hannah's father?"

"Not technically, no. But she doesn't know that and for a long time even Bill refused to believe it. By some strange pregnancy weirdness I didn't even look pregnant until I hit my sixth month." Levi looked like he wanted to say something so she hurried forward before he could stop her. It was hard enough to admit the depth of her poor choices and crappy judgment without interruption. "I met Bill not long after Seth's death and what can I say? I was young, scared and suddenly stupid. He offered comfort in what felt like a very cruel world and I grabbed it if only for a temporary respite. My one and only experience with a one night stand went weirdly awry. Bill kept coming around and I finally broke down and told him I was pregnant. I seriously think he believed it could be his no matter how much I told him differently. I should have taken that as a warning sign, but I didn't. I wanted to believe that everything would be all right. That somehow fate had stepped in and brought me someone who wanted to be a father. Hannah came along, he claimed her as his and life went on."

She closed her eyes and stopped talking. Part of her felt sick and part of her felt relief. She'd needed to tell someone for a very long time. Every person she'd ever met since Seth died, she'd wondered. What would they think of her if they knew the truth? Over the years she'd imagined many variations of disgust, revulsion and hatred her mind could conjure. All the things Bill claimed when he'd found her diary and read it from cover to cover. There were other words too but they were too vile even to contemplate.

"So that's why you freaked out when you thought I was doing the same kind of thing. Stepping in because Hannah needs a father?"

She hung her head and then nodded. She'd never forgive herself for not seeing the difference between Bill and Levi.

"When did Bennett find out Seth was your step brother?"

Tori's body jerked at the question. "The day he left. I have no idea why he'd decided to go through my old boxed up belongings that afternoon, but he did. By then he'd started working for one of the local churches as a youth minister and the change in him had been dramatic. He'd started going on long missionary trips and Hannah and I were seeing less and less of him all the time. Things were weird and I didn't know how to fix them.

"Oh shit. You didn't know about the others?"

She shook her head again. "I was naive to the end. Then he found out about Seth and could no longer stand the sight of a woman with no moral code or her inbred mongrel daughter."

Levi stood and headed toward the door. "That's it. I'm going to kill that no good piece of shit. Fucking scum."

She ran after him and grabbed his arm. "Don't. He isn't worth it."

Levi stood stock still and she could feel the tension

vibrating under the fingers wrapped around his forearm.

"Please. Hannah and I are better off without him. According to the news reports he is on his way to getting everything he deserves."

Levi turned her into his arms and gripped the sides of her face and brought her close. "But you are not better off without me. I don't care about any of this because everyone makes mistakes. Do you hear me? *Everyone.* Myself included. In retrospect I realize it was a little weird for me to think of you and Hannah when I drew up the plans for my renovation, but I wasn't planning anything nefarious. It was more like you were my inspiration. I couldn't get you out of my mind and that bled into the house plans. If it's too creepy, I'll sell it. Or I can hire a decorator to come in and make it look like the bachelor pad from hell. Whatever it takes I don't care. None of this matters because I still love you and I always will. You are my heart now. You and Hannah. You're just going to have to accept that you and her are a package deal. My package deal."

He kissed her hard and Tori couldn't breathe. Not that she cared. Tears were streaming down her cheeks and her fingers were curling tightly into the front of his shirt. When he finally broke free they were both panting and his fingers were brushing her tears as quickly as they fell.

"You love me?" The words still stunned her.

He shrugged. "Sometimes the most obvious things in life reach out and grab you by the throat in the blink of an eye. Those are the moments you don't walk away from. You, Catori Inola Ford are my moment."

When he lifted her into his arms and started carrying her to the back of the house she let out the breath she'd still been holding. She had no idea how this had happened, but finally she'd done something right.

"You just want my peach pie," she teased, so filled with joy she wanted to burst.

"There is definitely that." He threw her down on the bed and came over her. "But first," He nudged her shirt up with his nose, "you have some teasing to answer for."

EPILOGUE

Levi stood in the back of the room and away from the crowd as he waited impatiently for Tori to join them after her shift. No matter how hard he'd tried to convince her she didn't need to work at the restaurant or the club anymore, she'd insisted. Her only concession had been to accept a healthy raise and the ability to set her own schedule. And he got to spend as much time as he wanted to with Hannah while she worked.

Tonight, many of the members and most of his family had gathered in one of the 'members only' private playrooms of the third floor in Purgatory. There were St. Andrews crosses attached to the far wall, a couple of spanking benches in the back, and an assortment of comfortable chairs surrounded a small stage. That's where Tucker stood with Maggie, his submissive, by his side. They'd recently made up during one of her weekends home and he'd dragged her here under the guise of a make up scene. Levi instantly liked her the moment they met. He felt kind of bad now for the assumptions he'd made about her being a troublemaker. Although he'd still like to sit down with her and hear the story about her getting busted in a BDSM club raid. That sounded like one hell of a tale.

Mason and Nina were close by doing their best to ignore each other. Levi had yet to learn the strange back and forth relationship they had, but Tucker assured him they were quite close. He didn't see it, but was willing to take his brother's word for it.

The last few weeks had brought tense moments for the brothers as they awaited the decision on whether formal charges would be filed against Tucker's mother. Nina still remained distant although Tori mentioned she'd been spending some time with Gabe and they both wondered what that was about.

"Hey, Levi. Did I miss anything?"

Speak of the devil. "Nah. Nothing so far." He held out his hand and Gabe greeted him again with their old fraternity shake. It brought a smile to both their faces. Levi glanced behind his friend. "Where's Tori? She didn't come over with you?"

"Right behind me." Gabe drifted in the direction of Nina and Mason and he stood back to watch. When his friend made his presence known there was a distinct change in Nina's posture. Her muscles loosened and her face softened, she even smiled. Curious, Levi wanted to know more and made a mental note to talk to Gabe.

The music from downstairs was piped into this room and the hard driving rhythm of the music made his blood pulse. It had been too long since he and Tori had played in a space remotely like this and the desire to do so sounded like a great idea. She'd look amazing draped over one of the spanking benches with her ass high in the air for his pleasure. If only she'd get her cute butt in here. He smiled. Something about his woman made him infinitely impatient at times.

"They'd make a great couple, don't you think?"

Levi turned at the sound of Tori's voice, his body going on high alert and nearly swallowed his tongue. She stood next to him in a white skintight dress that left almost nothing to the imagination. Even in the dim mood lighting of the room he could see that the thin fabric would be sheer in more direct lighting. Her nipples were already hard, giving him nothing but ideas on how he could torture them again. Before he could greet her properly, Tucker started his speech.

"I'm really glad this is happening tonight. Everyone's been so stressed since the press conference," Tori whispered to Levi.

"Yes, they have. I wish I could say it was all over, but there are still some major problems to work through."

Tori squeezed his hand. "We'll get through it together. No matter what happens."

Levi groaned. "God, Tori. You just made me want you more and I didn't think that was possible." He leaned forward and gave her a quick hard kiss before returning his attention back to the stage. He didn't know how he was going to get through this event without having her.

Tucker got down on one knee and Maggie's hand flew to her mouth. I'm sure for Tucker that moment of shock made all of his scheming worth it. For Levi, all he could think about was Tori. Every time he inhaled he caught her scent. When Tucker asked Maggie to marry him all he heard was the sound of Tori's hitched breath as she brought her hand to her chest. His senses were on overload. The need he'd banked earlier returned in a full force of consumption. He needed to get her alone and out of that dress. *Now.*

The thought of getting her naked lead to him wondering if she wore panties underneath it. Did she finally succumb to his warning or would he have to tear another pair off of her? He pulled her close to his side and lowered his voice, "Tell me, my love, what exactly is under this dress?"

"Shhh," she warned. Then she looked at him with pure mischief coloring her face and shrugged.

He growled at her. "Then I guess I'll have to find out for myself." He shifted her slightly in front of him and edged his fingers underneath the ridiculously short thing that barely qualified as a dress even by his standards. One sudden move and half her ass would show. When his hand met a swath of lace a low grumble formed in his throat. He slid two fingers underneath the edge and wrapped his hand around the fabric.

"Oh my God. Levi, don't," Tori whispered, her voiced frantic.

"I warned you." Levi waited thirty seconds and Maggie squealed her acceptance from the stage to a round of raucous applause. During the commotion, Levi ripped the thin panties keeping him from the treasure he knew awaited.

Tori squeaked in surprise, but managed to keep calm for the most part. She only glanced around the room twice to see if anyone had noticed. Levi smiled and shoved the torn lace into his pants pocket. Later, they'd make a great restraint.

"Are you happy now?" Tori chided, her hip bumping against his.

"Almost." He groaned into her ear as he pushed two fingers between her legs and slid them through her wet sex. "Now I am," he growled.

"Shouldn't we be paying attention to Tucker and Maggie?" she asked, suddenly breathless.

"Not when all I can think about is you," he answered.

The barely there moan from Tori drove him even wilder. It didn't take much for her to draw the beast from within, but herculean effort on his part to restrain him. He moved his fingers in a slow rhythmic circle while keeping his eyes on the small crowd in front of them.

"We need to find a room of our own." She really had turned him into an animal.

In a turn of luck, Tucker finished his proposal and the rest of the invitees crowded around him. Taking that as his chance, Levi grabbed Tori's hand and fled the room. Levi rushed through the club corridor toward the Master's room. He doubted anyone would bother them there.

Impatient and greedy, Levi unlocked the door and dragged Tori inside.

"Levi," she started.

He shook his head. "Not going to stop now. Can't."

For a heartbeat they stared at each other before Levi whipped her around and attacked the zipper keeping that damned dress on her body. He peeled it off of her and stood frozen to the spot while staring at the curve of her back and the swell of her ass. His Catori would always be the most beautiful woman in his world.

He dropped to his knees and began kissing every inch of gorgeous bare skin. "I feel like the luckiest man in alive right now."

Tori spun and dropped down to meet him face to face. "Me. I'm the lucky one," she panted.

He smiled, nipping at her shoulder. "We'll just have to agree that were both pretty damned lucky." Her breasts rose and fell, pulling his attention to the perfect nipples that starred in pretty much all of his fantasies. Unable to resist, he reached out and rolled them both between his fingers. He worked her sensitive flesh until her mouth dropped open and she moaned.

"Mmm. You're so damned expressive. Amazing really."

"You play me so well," she smiled. "Hard to think straight when you do that."

He leaned forward and pressed his lips to the shell

of her ear. "Then don't think. Just feel." Levi changed tactics and pinched the tight buds until she gasped. Then he tightened his fingers some more.

"Oh, God, Levi--" She screamed long and loud.

Levi's mind broke as did the last of his restraint. He tore at his pants and freed his throbbing cock two seconds before he lifted her off the ground and pushed her back against the wall. Inches before he slammed into her, he stopped. He leaned slightly forward, his whole body shaking and nudged the tip of his cock at her entrance.

Her eyes flew open.

"Thank you, Catori."

"For what?" she gasped.

He slowly sank into her one lingering inch at a time. "For helping me find home."

***

After the champagne began to flow and he congratulated Tucker and his new fiancé, Mason left the party and slipped into his private dining room at Fire and Ice undetected. He studied the woman waiting for him as she stared out the third story window that overlooked one of the city's most popular green spaces. Rebecca's curly blonde hair hung loose and messy to her shoulders as if she'd finally given up the fight on keeping it under control. His mind wandered and he imagined his fingers grasping a handful as he entered her from behind...

In the window her curvy figure reflected back to him. Pulling at him like an irresistible magnet. She'd kept her attire professional with her typical work uniform with probably no idea the affect her simple pencil skirt and button down blouse had on him. His hands itched to turn her around and peel the silk shirt from her shoulders and place her lips on the satiny flesh underneath. They'd been skirting around the tension between them for weeks as they tap danced through her constant questions about his life and Purgatory.

Finally, he'd decided to broker a deal with the compelling woman. Which brought his gaze down to her ample backside that always made his dick stand at attention as more fantasies ran through his head. All of her insistent probing had given him more ideas than he could count, although to his credit he'd tried everything to resist her. But ultimately he'd given in to his obsession and offered her a contract.

In exchange for helping him with his publicity problems, she'd be given an exclusive interview and he'd take her under his wing and introduce her to her wildest submissive fantasies.

He'd loved the shocked look on her face. Even better the soft gasp he'd heard when he pushed the contract across the table and told her to read it before giving him an answer. That had been weeks ago. Chaos had descended on his entire family after the shocking press conference and subsequent fall out. After not hearing back from her, he'd feared she was no longer interested in his offer. With the news splashed everywhere, anything he offered wouldn't exactly be exclusive anymore. None of which diminished the burning desire to be her mentor.

This morning she'd called his secretary and asked for an appointment, citing an outstanding contract as her reason for the request. He'd instructed his secretary to book them for a late dinner at Fire and Ice.

He strode further into the room and wished he could read her thoughts. Her body language didn't give him any real clues. There was no obvious tension in the lines of her body, nor any noticeable fidgeting. Without seeing her face she appeared as cool and collected as always.

Except when she thought no one was watching her

observe at Purgatory. Those moments haunted him.

Everything logical in the world told him going forward with an agreement between them was a bad idea that could and likely would go horribly wrong at a moment's notice. Again, all useless warnings with her standing in the same room, breathing the same air. From the first moment she'd looked at him with soft, inquisitive eyes and he'd gotten the scent of her favored perfume, nothing but being inside her had mattered. In fact, he planned to get so deep inside her she'd forget everything but her submission. Whatever her goals for continuing to investigate Purgatory and its mysterious owners would no longer matter. She had the soul of a submissive that was like a blank black and white slate and he planned to fill in the colors.

Mason shifted his stance and walked further into the room. The longer he stood there and perved on her, the tighter his pants got. Time to get this meeting started.

"You're early," he said.

She turned, a startled look on her face. "I assumed you'd prefer punctuality."

A slow smile crossed his face. "You'd be correct, Miss Adams. Please, have a seat." He held out a chair at the table and waited for her to comply. She walked over and took a seat and Mason tried damn hard not to stare at her amazing legs he'd already imagined wrapped around him as he pushed in her chair.

He settled into the seat across from her and tried to remember that her goal in coming to his town had been to dig into his family's past. "I take it you've read through the contract?"

"I have," she answered.

"And? Are you here to accept it?" He'd waited long enough to hear her answer, he wouldn't beat around the bush now.

"That depends. I have a few questions." She tucked

her hair behind her ear and he couldn't help follow the finger trailing down her neck.

Mason leaned forward. "I figured you would. Feel free to ask whatever you'd like. I don't want there to be any confusion between us. Something like this isn't to be entered into lightly."

She tipped forward as well and leveled a stare in his direction. "There are many possibilities I could begin with. Especially when it comes to some of the activities you listed as requirements from a submissive. However, I prefer to get straight to the point and the most important question of them all."

He smiled again, anxious to hear what one question held that much importance to her. Not that his body cooperated much with his brain when it came to her. Before she could ask, he stood from his chair and pulled her from hers. Their bodies melded together. Just once he thought to himself before he slid his mouth across hers. To his delight, she didn't move. He licked over her bottom lip and then bit it lightly.

"Ask your question Miss Adams before it's too late," he prompted.

Her chest rose and fell as he waited.

"What happens when the contract ends?" she gulped for air. "I mean what *really* happens?"

###

FROM THE AUTHOR

Thank you so much for reading! I hope you enjoyed reading Levi's Ultimatum as much as I enjoyed writing it. I'm hard at work writing my next BDSM Romance, but while you are waiting I invite you to check out all the books I have available to read in the meantime. You can see the full list with links on the books page of my website at http://elizagayle.net

If you'd like to be notified when my next book comes out or when I run any contests, please sign up for my newsletter at the top of my website

If you enjoyed this book please take a moment to help other readers discover it by leaving a review and letting them know you liked *Levi's Ultimatum*. Reader reviews help others decide which books to buy and provide a learning opportunity for the author.

Looking for more Purgatory Club?

Here is the complete series order for both the Purgatory Club series and the Purgatory Masters:

Purgatory Club
ROPED
DISPLAYED
WHIPPED
BURNED
BOTTOMS UP

Purgatory Masters
TUCKER'S FALL
LEVI'S ULTIMATUM

CPSIA information can be obtained at www.ICGtesting.com
Printed in the USA
LVOW06s0957180514

386210LV00003BA/213/P